OUT IN THE OPEN

In a drought-stricken country ruled by violence, a young boy has fled his home. Crouched in his hiding place, he hears the shouts of the men hunting him. When the search party has passed, what lies before him is an infinite, arid plain, one he must cross in order to escape those from whom he's fleeing. One night he crosses paths with an old goatherd, and from that moment nothing will ever be the same for either of them . . .

JESÚS CARRASCO

◆

OUT IN
THE OPEN

Translated from the Spanish by
Margaret Jull Costa

Complete and Unabridged

ULVERSCROFT
Leicester

First published in Great Britain in 2016 by
Vintage
London

First Large Print Edition
published 2018
by arrangement with
Vintage
Penguin Random House
London

The moral right of the author has been asserted

A catalogue record for this book is available
from the British Library.

ISBN 978–1–4448–3621–9

Published by
F. A. Thorpe (Publishing)
Anstey, Leicestershire

Set by Words & Graphics Ltd.
Anstey, Leicestershire
Printed and bound in Great Britain by
T. J. International Ltd., Padstow, Cornwall

This book is printed on acid-free paper

To the memory of
Nicolás Carrasco Royano

1

From inside his hole in the ground, he heard the sound of voices calling his name, and, as if they were crickets, he tried to pinpoint the precise location of each man within the bounds of the olive grove. The desolate howling of fire-scorched scrub. He was lying on one side, knees drawn up to his chest, with barely enough room to move in that cramped space. His arms either around his knees or serving as a pillow, and only a tiny niche for his knapsack of food. He had made a roof out of pruned twigs which he had piled on top of two thick branches that served as beams. Tensing his neck, he raised his head so as to hear better and, half-closing his eyes, listened out for the voice that had forced him to flee. He didn't hear it, nor did he hear any barking, which was a great relief because he knew that only a well-trained dog could find him in his hiding-place. A gun dog or a truffle hound. Perhaps an English bloodhound, with sturdy legs and floppy ears, like the one he'd seen in a photo in a newspaper brought from the city.

Luckily for him, there were no such exotic

breeds where he lived. Only greyhounds. All skin and bone. Mystical creatures that raced after hares at top speed, never stopping to follow a scent because they had been put on earth with only one purpose in life: to pursue and capture. They had red lines emblazoned on their flanks, souvenirs of their masters' whips. The same whips that were used to beat into submission the children, women and dogs of that arid plain. Greyhounds, of course, could run, whereas he had to lie stock-still in his small clay cave. Lost among the hundreds of smells that the subterranean depths normally reserve for earthworms and the dead. Smells he should not be smelling, but which he himself had sought out. Smells that distanced him from his mother.

Whenever he saw greyhounds or thought of them, he always remembered a man who used to live in his village. A cripple who moved about the streets on a kind of tricycle propelled by a handle that he turned, bending over it like an organ-grinder. At dusk, he would leave the houses of the village behind him and travel the beaten paths heading north, the only ones his chariot could manage. The dogs escorted him, tethered with leads made of frayed string. It was painful to see him trundling along on his ramshackle machine, and the boy had often wondered why he didn't get the dogs to pull him. His classmates used to say that when the cripple had no further use for one of those dogs, he would hang it from an olive tree. In the boy's short life, he had seen dozens of dogs hanged by the neck from remote trees. Bags full of dislocated bones like giant chrysalises.

He sensed that the men were getting very close now and so he lay utterly still. He heard his name proliferating among the trees like drops of rain falling onto a sheet of water. Curled up in his hiding-place, he wondered if that would perhaps be his one reward: hearing his name called out again and again at daybreak among the olive trees. He recognised two voices, one belonging to the landlord of the local bar and the other to one of the muleteers who spent the summer in the village. And although he couldn't actually identify their voices, he imagined that the postman and the local basket-weaver would be there too. Down in the depths of his hole, he experienced an unexpected warm rush of joy. A kind of silent, childish jubilation that made his skin prickle. He wondered if they would put such effort into finding his brother. Would *he* have attracted such a large search party? Hearing that chorus of voices, he felt that he had perhaps revived some kind of community spirit and, for a moment, his bitterness withdrew into one small corner of his stomach. He had gathered around him all the men of the village, all the strong, weather-worn arms that tilled the fields and sowed the furrows with grain. He had caused an incident. Perhaps the need to come together had forced old enemies to roll up their sleeves and work alongside each other. He wondered if anything would remain of that moment in a few years or even weeks. If it would still be a topic of conversation as people left church or the local bar. Then he thought about his father and imagined him making his excuses to all and sundry. He saw him, as he so often had, feigning helplessness. Probably trying to make everyone believe that his son had fallen down some hidden well while chasing after a young partridge, that the family had once again been the victim of misfortune and that God had just torn from him flesh of his flesh. Even with his head pressed against his knees, the boy managed to shake it gently as if to chase away those thoughts. The image of his fawning, servile father came back to him, this time in the company of the bailiff. A scene which, like no other, provoked all kinds of chaotic feelings in his body. He listened as intently as he could for traces of the bailiff's voice, and even the

4

absence of that voice frightened him. He imagined him walking along, cigar in mouth, behind the line of men currently combing the olive grove. He would trample the clods of earth or bend indolently down to pick up the odd olive that had escaped the last harvest. His watch-chain poking out beneath his jacket. His brown felt hat, his bow tie, tight collar, moustache stiff with sugar water.

A man's voice just yards from the hole startled him from his thoughts. It was the schoolmaster. He was talking to another man some way off. The boy felt his heart beat faster, felt the blood hammering in his veins. After hours of immobility, the cramps in his muscles were urging him to leave his hiding-place. He considered bringing the whole situation and his discomfort to an immediate end. After all, he hadn't killed anyone, he hadn't stolen, he hadn't taken the name of God in vain. He was on the point of moving the twigs covering the hole in order to attract the attention of the men nearest to him. One of them would tell the other to be quiet and then turn his head so as to hear where exactly the noise had come from. Their eyes would meet. They would creep towards the pile of twigs, not knowing whether they would find a rabbit or the lost boy. Then they would move the twigs to one side and find him there, curled into a ball. He would pretend to be unconscious, and his unconscious state, along with the mud, wet clothes and dirty hair, would be his masterstroke. He would at least be assured of one moment of glory. Not that it would last, of course, more a case of feast today and starve tomorrow. Then, summoned by the men's shouts, the others would come running. His father would arrive, breathing hard, initially thrilled and happy. They would form a whirlpool of people around him that would barely let him breathe, like a newly struck match that struggles at first and shows no sign of becoming the mellifluous flame that will eventually consume the matchstick. They would disinter him amid shouts of joy. Around him, manly embraces would send up little clouds of dust as the searchers clapped each other on the back. Then, to the accompaniment of songs and warm wine, he would be carried to the village on a stretcher with his father's rough hand resting on his small, brown chest. A joyful exordium to a drama that would propel them all to the village bar and, later, to their respective houses. Afterwards, the only witnesses would be the thick stone walls that supported the roof and kept the rooms cool. A communal prelude to his father's worn leather belt. The swift copper-coloured buckle slashing dully through the fetid kitchen air. His earlier feigned state of unconsciousness getting its unjust deserts.

Almost immediately above him, he heard the sound of the schoolmaster blowing his nose. A loud, membranous explosion that used to make the teacher's clean handkerchief shiver and cause the children to break out in a sweat as they struggled to suppress their laughter. The shadow cast by the teacher's thin body loomed over the roof. He closed his eyes and clenched his teeth while the teacher peed onto the pile of twigs.

He allowed a long time to pass after the last voice had left the olive grove. He wanted to be quite sure that he would find no one there when he did finally lift the lid on his refuge, and he had determined to wait for as long as was necessary. Nothing, not even the hours spent underground or the teacher's urine still sticky in his hair or the hunger which was, for the first time, pricking him hard, nothing was enough now to weaken his resolve, because the black flower of his family's betrayal still gnawed at his stomach. He fell asleep.

★   ★   ★

When he woke, the sun was already high in the sky. The harsh noonday glare pierced the twig roof, faintly illuminating his knees with dusty needles of light. As soon as he opened his eyes, he was aware of the numbness in his muscles and realised that his own body had woken him from his slumbers. He reckoned he must have spent seven or eight hours in that hole and resolved to get out as soon as possible. He cautiously raised his head and felt his hair touch the roof. He sat up, pushed aside some of the twigs and peered about him, his neck as stiff as a rusty hinge, to make sure no one was there. He could leave now and head towards the north; he knew of a spring where the muleteers watered their mules, his plan being to hide among the reeds, wait until no one was looking, then smuggle himself aboard the cart of some trader, hide away among the frying pans and knickers, and wait until they were many miles from the village and it was safe to come out. He knew, though, that in order to reach that spring, he would have to walk through open countryside in broad daylight with only a few piles of rocks as shelter. Any local shepherd or hunter would be sure to identify his scrawny body as that of the lost boy, so his only alternative was to remain hidden until evening, when his wiry limbs could pass for a withered bush or some vague, dark shape silhouetted against the setting sun. He carefully replaced the twigs and crouched down again.

During his self-imposed imprisonment, he became familiar with his various companions in the hole: beetles, earwigs and, especially, earthworms. He felt behind him for the hollow he had made for his knapsack. He opened the canvas bag, took out a piece of sausage and chewed it slowly. He drank some warm water from the small wineskin that had grown as swollen as a dead cat after the several days it had remained hidden prior to his escape. It was not long before he felt his bladder fill up and become painfully distended. His hunched position put further pressure on it, and a few drops of urine occasionally leaked out, only increasing his discomfort. When the stabbing pains became unbearable, he tried to pull down his trousers. He struggled with his flies and his belt, but there was so little space, he could barely move. He considered climbing out of the hole for a moment, but was afraid of being spotted from a distance or of leaving some trace, however small, for the search party that was doubtless still searching for him. After a while, he managed to slide his trousers down over his bottom. He tried to push his penis back between his legs, away from his body, but so cramped was his hiding-place that he immediately became aware that his foreskin was touching his ankles and, at that point, he could hold it in no longer and simply let himself go like a wheel rolling downhill, He had spent so many hours lying in the hole that the compacted clay had become like a bowl in which the urine formed a puddle. The sulphurous atmosphere turned his refuge into a toxic pot. He reached up with his head towards the roof, pressing his mouth against the gaps between the twigs, trying to gulp down some fresh air from outside. He needed to escape, to burst through the roof and out into the olive grove as if his body were a cork suddenly liberated from the depths of a lake. He closed his eyes and clung to the roots reaching down into the hole. He lay for a long time, unaware of the tension in his muscles, and then, when he did become conscious of it, a sudden weariness overwhelmed him and his muscles relaxed, allowing his body to settle back into the shape of the pit. The damp heat in the hole dazed him, and the softened clay beneath the small of his back produced in him a kind of dull discomfort, a drowsiness that led him into sleep.

★ ★ ★

The light coming in through the roof had faded almost to nothing when he was woken by the sound of rustling leaves. Some small rodent, he thought. He desperately needed to uncurl, to breathe freely, to shake off the mud covering skin and clothes, to dry his trousers, to get out of there. He must first make sure, though, that the noise that had woken him was not some kind of threat. He sat up and, very carefully, with the top of his head, lifted the roof of branches just enough to create a gap through which he could see. Only a few inches from where he was hiding, a field mouse was snuffling around in the curled leaves fallen from the olive trees. Then he painstakingly dismantled his roof branch by branch, twig by twig, like nest-building in reverse. He peeped out, turning his head this way and that like a periscope until he had scanned the whole of the olive grove and found no signs of life apart from that field mouse, now scampering away past the piles of prunings. By the time he emerged from the hole, the light had taken on a dusty, reddish quality. There was no sun on the horizon, but a yellowish glow lit the plain from the west, casting long shadows over the fallow fields. He stretched his body in every possible direction: squatting down, standing up, stamping his feet, and, for a moment, he completely forgot he was on the run and didn't even notice the geometric fragments of mud that detached themselves from the soles of his shoes. His trousers were still wet. He stood with legs apart and unstuck the fabric from his skin. If he had run away in winter, he thought, it would have frozen to him.

He had chosen that place months before because it was the wooded area nearest to the village. At the time, he didn't know at what hour of the night he would be able to leave his house, nor how much time he would have to reach his hiding-place. If he fled in any other direction, the men would be able to spot him from hundreds of yards away. At least there he had the protection of the olive trees. Within the grove itself he had chosen the northern edge, because that would afford him the clearest view of the plain he would have to cross.

He took off his clothes and draped them over some low branches so that they would dry in the air. His skin felt swollen and uncomfortable. Wood pigeons were fluttering about in the tops of the trees, hoping to find a roosting place for the night. He rubbed his body with dry earth as if he were an elephant and immediately felt better. He removed his knapsack from the hole and walked the length of the olive grove until he found a suitable tree. He sat down naked on the ground and leaned his back against the knotty trunk.

Small stones stuck to his buttocks and the bark pricked his back. Once he had made himself relatively comfortable, he felt in his knapsack and took out a piece of hard cheese and a crust of stale bread. He ate the cheese and watched as the night gradually took possession of the earth. Above him, the pigeons were cooing. He gnawed at the skin of the cheese. When he had eaten it down to the rind, he was about to throw the rind away, but something stopped him: the memory of those men's voices calling him. He turned and glanced back into the olive grove, imagining the dark figures of the search party, silently shouting his name. He put the cheese rind back in the, knapsack. He was still hungry, though, and again rummaged among the contents, knowing full well that, once he had eaten the cheese, all he had left was half a dry sausage. He took it out and held it to his nose. Closing his eyes, he allowed himself to be filled by the scents of pepper and cinnamon. He licked the sausage and was about to bite into it, but again he felt the shadows of those men pursuing him and had no option but to keep the sausage for some time of greater need, which, he was sure, would not be long in coming.

He spent a long while running his tongue over his gums to allay the burning sensation left by the cheese. He bit off a chunk of bread, drank water from the wineskin, then lay down on the ground, resting his head on a tree root. The sky was a dark, dark blue. Up above, the stars were like jewels encrusted in a transparent sphere. The plain that lay stretched out before him gave off a smell of parched earth and dry grass as it slowly recovered from the rigours of the sun. A grey owl flew over his head and disappeared among the trees. This was the first time he had been this far from the village. What lay ahead was, quite simply, unknown territory.

2

He was heading north in the middle of the night, trying to avoid any existing paths. His trousers were still slightly damp, but this didn't bother him now. He was walking across the fallow fields, taking care to step only on the stubble left from the last harvest. The occasional partridge flew up as he passed, and he heard the sound of hares fleeing from the crunching sound made by his boots. Once he was out of the olive grove, his one plan was to keep going. He could recognise the Milky Way, the W of Cassiopeia and the Great Bear. From there, he could locate the Pole Star and that was where he was directing his feet.

Although he had not as yet spent one whole day on the run, he knew that more than enough time had passed for fear already to be racing through the village streets towards his parents' house, an invisible torrent that would carry all the women of the village along with it to form a pool around his mother, who would be lying limply on her bed, her face as wrinkled as an old potato. He imagined the turmoil in the house and in the village. People perched on the stone bench outside, hoping to catch a glimpse through the half-open door of what was going on inside. He could see the bailiff's motorbike parked outside: a sturdy machine with a sidecar on which he drove through the village and the surrounding fields, leaving dust and noise in his wake. The boy knew that sidecar well. He had often travelled in it, covered by a dusty blanket. He recalled the greasy smell of the wool and the cracked, oilcloth edging. To him, the roar of that engine was like the trumpet sounded by the first Angel, the angel who had mingled fire and blood and cast it down upon the earth until all the green grass was burned up.

The bailiff was the only person in the region to own a motorised vehicle, and the governor was the only one to own a vehicle of the four-wheeled variety. He himself had never seen the governor, but had heard hundreds of accounts of the time he came to the village for the inauguration of the grain silo. Apparently, he was welcomed by children waving little paper flags, and several lambs were sacrificed in celebration. Those who had been there described the car as if it were a magical object.

★ ★ ★

Tiny and dark in the midst of that still-greater darkness, he wondered if he might find something useful on the imaginary line he was following due north. Perhaps some fruit trees along the road or fountains of clean water or endless springtimes. He couldn't really come up with any concrete expectation, but that didn't matter. By heading north, he was travelling away from the village, away from the bailiff and from his father. He was on the move, and that was enough. The worst thing that could happen, he thought, would be to exhaust his limited strength by going round in a circle or, which came to the same thing, returning to his family. He knew that by keeping on in the same direction, sooner or later he would come across someone or something. It was just a matter of time. He might walk right round the world and end up back in his village, but, by then, it wouldn't matter. His fists would be as hard as rocks. More than that, his fists would *be* rocks. He would have wandered almost eternally and, even if he met no one else, he would have learned enough about himself and the earth for the bailiff never to be able to have him in his power again. He wondered if he would ever be capable of forgiving. If, once he had crossed the icy Pole, penetrated dense forests and traversed other wildernesses, the flame that had burned him inside would still be burning. Perhaps, by then, the desperation that had driven him from the home God had intended for him would have dissipated. It might be that distance, time and ceaseless contact with the earth would have smoothed away his rough edges and calmed him down. He remembered the cardboard globe at school. The large sphere wobbled about on its rickety wooden stand, but it was easy enough to find their village on it, because, year upon year, the fingers of several generations of children had worn away the spot, indeed, had erased the whole country and the surrounding sea.

★ ★ ★

In the distance, he could make out what appeared to be a bonfire and he wondered how far away it was. He stopped and tried to calculate, but in the indecipherable darkness, it was impossible to judge. What he imagined to be a distant bonfire could just as easily, he thought, be the flame of a match only a few yards ahead or even a whole house ablaze miles away.

Like an Indian dazzled by the glittering trinkets offered him by a conquistador, he headed towards that one luminous point. For more than an hour he tramped over clods of earth and over stones. The wind was in his face, which meant that if the person who had lit the fire owned dogs, they would only notice his presence if he made a noise. He had no clear objective in approaching that point of light. The fire might belong to a shepherd, a muleteer or a bandit. He hoped that, as he approached, the light from the fire would bring him the necessary information. The idea of coming face-to-face with a criminal terrified him, and who knows what mangy dogs would be sleeping around that fire? On the other hand, he did know that he was going to need food and water from whoever had lit that fire. Whether he would ask for it or be obliged to steal it was something he would decide when he knew just who it was he was dealing with. He heard a chorus of what sounded like tinkling bells coming from that direction and this reassured him. He still took extreme caution when covering the last few yards, placing his feet as gently on the ground as if he were walking on a bed of rose petals. Shortly before he reached the encampment, he found a clump of prickly pears and hid behind them to observe the scene.

On the other side of the fire, facing the flames, a man was lying on the ground, although the boy still couldn't tell how old he was because a blanket covered his whole body, from top to toe. A gentle glow, like a distant ember, was beginning to appear above the horizon, revealing the shapes of trees that the night had kept hidden. He thought he could make out several poplar trees and assumed that the herd of goats was there for the same reason that the trees were. A goat emerged out of the darkness and walked behind the goatherd before disappearing into the pre-dawn shadows. Its bell drew a line of sounds in the air like a piece of knotted string. To one side lay a donkey, its legs folded meekly beneath its chest. Scattered around, he could see the motionless bodies of goats, which would doubtless soon wake up. At the man's feet lay a bag and a small dog curled up asleep.

The now faint light from the fire made the shadows dance like black flames. The boy peered round the cactus plant, trying to get a better look at the man. Something pricked his arm and he drew back. The buckle on his knapsack clinked. The dog immediately opened its eyes and pricked up its ears, then got to its feet, sniffing the air in all directions. The boy kept a firm grasp on his arm, as if the treacherous limb had a life of its own and was again about to hurl itself against the cactus spines. The dog began to move towards him, keeping close to the goatherd at first, then widening the radius of its search and slowly getting nearer to where he was standing. Watching the dog approach, the boy did not think it seemed terribly fierce, but he knew that one can never trust that kind of dog. In the village, people called them *garulos*: mongrels, which, through years of cross-breeding, had grown ever smaller, any distinctive racial characteristics now an unrecognisable blur. When the dog was just a few feet away, it stopped and focused all its senses on the clump of prickly pears. It again sniffed the air, and then, for some reason, relaxed and walked all around the intruder's hiding-place, wagging its tail and clearly curious. When it discovered him, it showed no alarm and did not even bark. On the contrary, it went over and licked the placatory hand the boy had held out to keep it from barking. With that gesture, the boy's fear of betrayal evaporated. It was as if the smells of earth and urine with which he was impregnated brought him closer to the world of the dog. He grabbed its head in his two hands and stroked it under the chin. For a while, the boy kept the dog quiet with his caresses, the time it took to decide whether or not to cover the few yards separating him and the bag lying at the man's feet.

He opened his own knapsack and took out the remaining half-sausage — all he had left. Leaving the dog busily gnawing at the dried meat, he emerged from his hiding-place and began to creep towards the bag. The light from the fire cast a gothic shadow over the prickly pears behind him.

As he approached, he felt afraid and would have liked to go back where he came from, to withdraw to some safe place and wait for daylight in order to reconsider his options. However, behind the prickly pears, the dog was devouring the only food he had and he knew there was no turning back.

He returned to his first plan, as simple as it was terrifying. He would go over to the bag and gently drag it towards him by the strap amidst a surrounding chorus of bleating. He would definitely not attempt to uncover the man's face, because that would be both wrong and provocative. Apart from the food that the dog was now eating, he had never stolen from an adult and was only doing so now because he had no alternative. At home, the very stones of the walls were the guardians of an ancestral law according to which children must keep their eyes firmly fixed on the ground whenever they were caught doing something they shouldn't. They must present their executioner with the back of their neck as meekly as if they were sacrificial offerings or propitiatory victims. Depending on the seriousness of the crime, a slap on the back of the neck might be all the punishment they got or, equally, it could merely be the preamble to a far worse beating.

Standing very near the man now, he was again gripped by doubt and even considered not stealing the bag. He would simply wait by the fire until the man woke up. Then he would reveal himself to him as he was: a defenceless, unthreatening child. With luck, he thought, the man wouldn't be from around there, but had come in the hope of finding some stubble for his goats. Accustomed to solitude, he might even be grateful for some company. The man would offer him a little food and something to drink, then each would go his own way.

Suddenly, he heard a snort immediately behind him and was petrified. He didn't move. All his strength vanished into the void that fear had opened up before him. The goatherd disappeared, along with the bag and the herd of goats, swallowed up by the darkness where his mind had once been. He trembled and his stomach gurgled into life again as he felt something hard pressing against the small of his back and, despite himself, turned round. The dog was poking him with its nose. Between its teeth it was carrying the piece of string from one end of the sausage. The boy took a deep breath, knelt down on the ground and returned to his task.

The bag was made of thick leather. It smelled of dried onions and sweat. He hooked two fingers round the strap and gave a gentle tug. When he felt the weight of the bag, he threw all caution to the wind. His mind filled up with images of food, and everything around him was replaced by what he imagined to be the contents of that bag. He managed to drag his booty a few inches more in almost absolute silence until one particularly greedy tug sent the stiff body of the bag — as if it were a drum skin — thudding over the pebbles.

'Where do you think you're going with that?'

He froze at the sound of the gruff voice coming from the other side of the fire, which lit up the grimace of fear that was now his face, the face of a silent-film actor or a child caught red-handed for the first time.

'I'm hungry, sir.'

'Didn't anyone teach you to ask nicely?'

At that moment, he would have liked

simply to run away with the bag and leave the man there, talking from underneath his blanket. He wondered if perhaps the dog was not as friendly as it had seemed. He knew nothing as yet of loyalties or of the time that passes between man and beast, knitting them together ever more tightly.

'Help me up, boy.'

The boy dropped the leather strap and approached hesitantly. A couple of yards away, he stopped and studied the man's body. His face was still covered by the blanket, but his legs were now visible from the knees down. The man stirred feebly beneath his blanket, perhaps trying to fasten his trousers or feeling for his lighter in order to light his first cigarette of the day, and by the time his head appeared, the boy was once more hidden behind the prickly pears. In the time he remained there, the very faintest glimmer of light began to illumine a few corners of the encampment. He saw that he had been right in thinking that the trees were poplars and could see the effects of the drought on their topmost leaves. He counted nine nanny goats and one billy goat. He also noticed a construction he hadn't seen before: a kind of pyramid-shaped shack made out of branches cut from the nearby trees. From its walls hung straps, ropes, chains, a metal milk churn and a blackened frying pan. It was more like a tabernacle than a shelter. Separating the hut from the poplar trees was a woven fence held up by four posts hammered into the ground.

The goatherd had by then sat up and rolled himself a cigarette. It took him several minutes to get to his feet because the blanket had become tangled around his legs and elbows. Although the boy could still not really make out the man's features, he assumed from the way he moved that he was old. A scrawny old man who slept in his clothes. A dark jacket with wide lapels, a dishevelled mop of grey hair and what looked like a white brush stroke that covered his face from his nose downwards.

The goatherd saw the boy reappear from behind the prickly pear, but barely noticed him because he was too busy blowing on the wick of his rope lighter. When the boy was about six feet away from the man, he stopped. From that distance, he could see the goatherd's hair full of straw, and the holes in the elbows of his jacket. He was sitting on the ground with the blanket covering his legs, and the boy was surprised that he could sit comfortably like that, his back bent. The old man glanced up and sat staring at the boy. He had placed his cigarette behind one ear and was cupping the orange rope wick with the palm of one hand. Then the goatherd made a gesture that the boy would often see him make in the weeks to come. With the tips of thumb and index finger he wiped away the saliva from the corners of his mouth. Then he did the same with just his index finger, as if to smooth aside any hairs from his unruly moustache.

'Sit down, it's time to eat.'

The man pointed to a spot near his feet, and the boy did as he was told. For a while, the goatherd continued flicking the wheel of his rope lighter and unsuccessfully blowing on the wick. The boy watched in silence, mouth half-open, astonished at the old man's inepitude, for sometimes he missed the wheel altogether or failed to strike it hard enough. The boy's hands began moving of their own accord because he had often used such a lighter himself.

When the old man finally managed to light the cigarette and take his first few puffs, he rested his free hand on the ground and relaxed his shoulders as if he had just completed a very necessary task. He pursed his lips and whistled, and the dog got up and ran to the place where the goats were already beginning to stir. The dog immediately rounded up a group of brown goats and brought them over to where the man was sitting. Without even getting up, the man used his crook to hook a goat round one of its hind legs and drag it towards him. Then, keeping a firm grip on the animal with one hand, he pushed the blanket aside and drew in his legs. The boy watched this manoeuvre, surprised at the old man's sudden show of agility, given that only a moment before, it had taken him an age simply to light a cigarette. When the goatherd had the rear end of the goat in front of him, he placed a metal saucepan underneath its udders. The first drops fell, tinkling, into the pan. When he had enough milk, he gave the goat a slap and it skittered off to rejoin its fellows. Then he held out the pan to the boy, but when the boy didn't move, he set it down on the ground and continued smoking his cigarette.

They sat in silence, gnawing on wedges of greasy cheese, strips of dried meat and a little stale bread. The goatherd took long swigs from his wineskin, and the boy wondered when the man would ask who he was and what he was doing there. He was afraid that news of his disappearance might also have reached this part of the plain, because he was all too aware that, however arduous his adventure had proved up until now, he was still not that far from the village. At one point, it occurred to him that the old man's welcome could be a trick to hold him there while he waited for the search party or even for the bailiff himself to arrive. In that case, he knew exactly what he would do. He would run back to the clump of prickly pears and crouch down among them. The horses would paw the ground around the cactus spines, but would not dare to come near. If the search party wanted to take him home, they would have to drag him out. They would have to risk tearing their shirts and getting scratched or else, still mounted, riddle him with bullets and then, finally, kill the only witness.

When the old man had finished his breakfast, he reached into a pannier and brought out a crumpled sheet of newspaper. He used this to wrap up some food and then offered the package to the boy, who sat staring back at him. When the goatherd grew tired of holding out his arm, he did as he had with the saucepan of milk, and put the package down on the ground. He stowed the rest of the food in the pannier and again asked the boy to help him up. The boy went over and it was only then that he became aware of the mixture of aromas emanating from the man's body: the sickly aura of wine that hung around his head and mouth and the stench of dried sweat given off by his leathery skin. When the man stood up, he wasn't much taller than the boy. His trousers were tied around the waist with a piece of string, and his boots looked as if they were made of cardboard. After helping him to his feet, the boy took a few steps back and stood watching the man, who was becoming more agile with each passing minute. The boy was again surprised by the ease with which he bent down to retrieve the blanket and fold it up. With the blanket over his arm, the old man whistled to the dog, which sprang to its feet and ran off to where the other goats were grazing.

The old man went over to the pyramid-shack and reached in through an opening in the branches that served as an entrance. He returned carrying a cork stool and a metal bucket. He took down the milk churn from where it hung on the wall and carried everything over to a small square enclosure. The dog had gathered the goats together and, by dint of barking and snapping at their heels, was herding them towards his master. When they had all arrived, the man removed one post from the corner of the corral fence, creating an opening through which he shooed in the goats. When they were all inside, he replaced the pole and joined it to its neighbour with the thick wire loop attached to one of them. Crammed in together, the goats were bleating furiously and trying to clamber on top of each other, resembling nothing so much as a pot of boiling stew.

The goatherd placed the bucket next to the section of fence that had served as a gate. The bucket was as wide at the bottom as it was at the top, and reminded the boy of the one they used at home to empty the latrine. The old man made sure the base was firmly embedded in the dusty ground, then from inside the bucket he took an adze and three rusty rods. He cleaned the mud off the blunt side of the blade and began hammering the rods into the ground very close to the outer edge of the bucket. When he had finished, he checked again to make sure that the bucket, like an encrusted jewel, would not move. He placed the stool so that it was facing the bucket and sat down. The boy had observed these comings and goings as if he were witnessing some vision of Our Lady. Open-mouthed, eyes lowered. The only part of his anatomy that moved was his head, which turned from side to side as he followed the goatherd's every manoeuvre.

Sitting on the stool, the old man again lifted one of the posts in the fence to create a narrow opening. He reached in and grabbed a goat by its leg, dragged it out and positioned it with its rear end over the bucket.

He then grasped the animal's teats and began milking. While he was working, he gazed up at the sky, as if checking for signs of rain. Echoing the old man's movements from afar, the boy also scanned the sky. Above their heads, the heavens were growing brighter, the glow slowly dousing the last and brightest stars. The sun, still lingering behind the hills in the east, would soon appear. Not a trace of cloud in the sky.

The boy looked back at the goatherd, who now had his head almost pressed against the animal's rear end and was briskly squeezing and pulling at the teats. The old man seemed nervous. When the goat, grown restless, kicked at the bucket and tried to run away, the old man tethered her back legs to two of the rods, only untethering her when he had finished milking. The goat then fled over to the poplars, where she reassured herself by nibbling the tips of the lowest branches.

One by one, all the goats came to the milking pail. As the boy watched it filling up, he wondered what the goatherd could possibly do with so much milk in the middle of that wilderness. When he'd finished, the old man got up and carried the bucket over to the churn, poured the milk into it and put the lid on. That was when he turned and spoke to the boy.

'You know, it's all the same to me if you've run away or if you're simply lost.'

The remark caught the boy unawares, and he shrank back. There was a long silence.

'Some men will be coming soon to collect the milk.'

3

The boy spent the rest of the morning in the sparse shade of a withered almond tree, a solitary example that had sprung up on an old boundary line between two now abandoned ploughed fields. From there, he had a panoramic view of the surrounding area and, should the search party come in sight, he could easily hide, or even escape, by crawling along that boundary. A few yards from where he was sitting, the path that had led him to that place continued downhill in a northerly direction. During the time he'd been sitting there, he'd travelled that path over and over with his eyes. To the right, an abandoned olive grove. Beyond that, a descending curve that skirted a small hill topped by a palm tree and, a little further off, what seemed to be a fig tree. And beyond that, the road appeared and disappeared among the waves of landscape until it vanished completely behind the last hill a couple of miles to the north.

He thought back to his meeting with the goatherd: the dog sniffing his hand and the man sitting smoking, bent-backed, his blanket over his legs. At midday, a drop of sweat trickled down his forehead and onto his trousers, where it dried instantly. He took off his shirt, laid it out before him and emptied onto it the contents of his canvas bag. He separated his belongings from the provisions given to him by the old man: three strips of dried goat's meat as taut as a barber's razor strop, a bit of cheese rind to gnaw on, a piece of bread and an empty tin. 'It will come in useful,' the man had said in the morning, throwing it at his feet.

'It will come in useful,' the boy repeated to himself as he sat there in the light shade. Why didn't he just give him some water? Were the springs so plentiful in the area that he assumed even a child like him would find them? Or was it an invitation to come back? Would he drink milk in it the next time they saw each other?

Thirst.

When the sun was at its highest point, he put everything back in the bag, pulled on his shirt and set off along the path. He walked as far as the bend and, before it continued downhill, he left the rutted track and climbed the hill to the palm tree. Its trunk was full of holes and up above hung a great dewlap of dead branches. The shade from the tree cast a dark stain on the earth, with the trunk at its centre. He put down his knapsack and cleared the leaves and stones from a patch of ground. Just as he had earlier, he took off his shirt and placed it like a tablecloth on the cleared area. Taking the food from his bag, he arranged it on the cloth and sat down to eat. He gnawed at the cheese rind, trying to drive from his mind the thought that he had no water. The greasy, rancid cheese formed a film on the roof of his mouth and would not let him rest because only water could wash away the sour taste it left behind. Still vainly rubbing at it with the tip of his tongue, he stood up. He inspected the ruins of an old adobe house so eroded by sun and wind that a low rectangle of mud bricks was all that remained of its walls. He could still make out the plan of the house which, like most houses in the province, had only one room, and this made him think of his own house on the outskirts of the village.

Now, alone beneath the sun, he contemplated the four-cornered crater formed by those low, blunt perimeter walls, barely a foot or so high. He climbed onto one of the walls and looked about him for anything that might betray the presence of his pursuers or indeed anyone else. The land, shimmering in the heat haze, undulated innocently away in all directions.

He looked, too, for some sign of a well. He

imagined that whoever had built the house must have done so near a spring or some underground stream. Without realising it, and keeping his eyes fixed on the ground, he gradually widened the radius of his explorations as far as the fig tree he had first noticed when he was sitting under the almond tree. He was surprised that it still had green leaves at that time of the year and did not smell of parched grass. Entranced by the sweet scent of the absent figs, a small, unconscious part of him allowed itself to be lulled into summoning up a pleasant memory. A summer afternoon perhaps, when he played beneath the fig tree at the railway station, at some still unsullied moment in his life. Hidden among the tender branches and the ripe figs. Drunk on the cavernous, labyrinthine abundance of the fruit's warm flesh. The changing colours as the figs ripened, their thin skin like a delicate frontier or a feeble façade created by the midsummer heat and intended to last only until touched.

He paused briefly beneath the perfumed shade and continued his search. Behind the fig tree he found the skeleton of a metal tower lying on the ground. Squares of rusted iron riveted together, at one end of which he could make out the rings that must once have supported the wooden arms. He thought it must be some kind of wind pump. He gave the structure a gentle kick, and the whole thing collapsed. At first, he couldn't understand why he hadn't noticed these remains from his viewing point beneath the almond tree, but seeing this heap of rust and iron smeltings from close to, what really surprised him was that anyone would have built such a small tower. Had it been a few feet taller, it might have caught some of the higher winds, which would have turned its arms faster and thus worked better for the farmer and his family. They might not then have had to leave, and that small heap of crumbling adobe would still be a home. He wondered how they hadn't realised something so obvious, and his first thought was that the farmer had perhaps run out of metal. Why then did he not use wood? How could anyone so unimaginative settle in a place like that? To judge by the state of the structure, his solution to the problem had arrived many years too late, and besides, who would have consulted a mere boy about how high to build a wind pump?

The feeling of his tongue sticking to the roof of his mouth brought him back to reality. He had come there in search of water. Near where the wind pump should have stood, he found the remains of a dead fig tree growing up between the bars of an iron grating. Given the abundance of tangled branches, growing thick and fat through the interstices of the grating and merging seamlessly with each other as if they were made of jelly, he deduced that there had once been plenty of water beneath its roots. He inspected every inch of this strange beast — half-tree, half-grating — until he found an as yet uncolonised gap in the rusty metal. He tried to look through the gap, but could see nothing, although he did feel a cool, damp breeze blowing up from the darkness below. Perhaps, despite everything, he was in luck. Had the goatherd intended to guide him to that spot when he gave him the tin?

He picked up a small pebble and dropped it in. The stone did not take long to reach the bottom, but for the boy, hoping to hear the sound of clear, fresh water, the time it took stretched out long after the stone had reached its destination. He dropped in another pebble and waited, with all his five senses alert. From the bottom there came only a dull thud. Not the plop or splash one would expect from a Well full of water. There was no sound either of stone hitting stone, and the boy decided that the bottom of the hole must be covered in the sticky mud left behind by some retreating subterranean stream.

Feeling flushed and agitated, he returned to the palm tree. His shirt was no longer in the shade. The cheese rind lay sweating on the cloth, leaving a large grease stain on it shaped like a coral reef. The tin was scalding hot and only the strips of meat seemed to have survived being left out in the sun. He stuffed the food back in his bag, put on his shirt and prepared to rest in the sparse shade and wait for the noonday heat to abate.

The hours passed slowly, but despite his hunger, he didn't touch the food, because he knew that eating would only make him thirstier. Again and again, the image of the water butt they had at home came into his mind. They used it to collect rainwater from the roof on the days when there was any rain. Even though it often didn't rain for months, the barrel was always full. His mother would go to the pump in the square carrying a three-gallon pitcher so that the water level in the butt never went below a mark cut into the inside of the barrel. This was an order issued by his father. She would go to the village square and walk along the line of pitchers left by the other women, all waiting their turn. When she reached the end of the line, she would set down her pitcher and return to the house to get on with her work. Every now and then, she would go back to where she had left the pitcher and move it closer to the pump as the pitchers ahead of hers were filled and taken away. And although almost all the pitchers had sprung from the hands of the same potter, everyone knew who each pitcher belonged to. The women who passed each other in the narrow streets would exchange murmured comments about how the line of pitchers was doing or whether the flow of water from the pump had improved. In summer, the flow — feeble at the best of times — would become a pathetic, infuriating trickle. And yet his mother still went to the pump every time the water in the butt sank lower than it should. He still remembered the afternoon when his father had burst into the room where they were sitting, grabbed his wife by the elbow and dragged her outside. He had stood her in front of the water butt, shaking her, before taking out his knife. His mother had opened her mouth, then buried her face in the folds of her black headscarf. With the point of his knife, his father had made a deep incision in the inside wall of the butt, then stormed off. Left alone, his mother had then slumped against the body of the barrel and slid to the ground. A little sawdust had remained floating on the surface of the black water.

Gazing up at the motionless fronds of the

palm tree silhouetted against the blue sky, he wondered about his father's need to hoard water. Perhaps he was storing it up in order to sell it at a premium when the pump did finally run dry. Perhaps he wanted to protect his family in case there was another drought and he became the last man to leave the village. He had inscribed his domination of his wife on the inside of the wooden barrel, like an open wound to which slimy bits of algae attached themselves. A hidden mark or a secret code. A gash that was like a dagger held to his mother's throat.

Even though he had walked all night, the boy knew that he mustn't fall asleep. The sun would set eventually, but as it progressed, the shade would shift too, leaving him exposed. He lay down on the easternmost side of the shade, thinking that he would change position as the shadow passed over him. He raised his head and looked around so as to calculate where he would end his reptilian advance. Then he lay down again and allowed himself to be lulled by the rattle of the dry palm leaves rustling up above.

He fell asleep.

When he woke, he had been lying in the sun for nearly two hours. His skin, from his chin to his scalp, felt strangely taut. Every hair follicle quivered with microscopic anguish, which, multiplied a hundredfold, provoked in him a feeling of stiff bewilderment. His brain burned and buzzed with a kind of cobalt-blue electricity and his head felt as if it were about to explode. He crawled on all fours into the shade and flopped down, sending up a miniature cloud of dust.

In his delirium, a rubbery web of curves is swaying and hovering above an oily surface. There is no horizon to speak of, but somewhere a source of reddish light is slowly disappearing. Darkness is winning the battle. All shades and nuances are disappearing, every cerebral cell is gradually closing down, until one convolution of his brain stirs back into life, creating an embryonic state of alert. His will, like Laocoön struggling against the serpents, is battling to forge a path into his consciousness through the damp penumbra of his brain. He or someone living inside him has sat down on the sella turcica of his skull and taken control of his body. He activates the organs and opens taps so that the blood can once more flow through the channels that had fallen in upon themselves during that sudden temporary void. The boy sitting in the seat orders him to open his eyes, but he can't because his eyelids won't lift. A strange, minuscule wave passes over his forehead like a sheet of sticky sandpaper abrading his tender skin. Again he tries to open his eyes, but without success. His eyelids weigh as heavy as curtains made of embossed leather. Infernal screams push the walls of his brain inwards. He feels a pounding in his translucent temples and his eyes bob about in their sockets like ice cubes in a glass. The person sitting inside his brain is searching for alternatives. He travels through his hollow body as far as his fingertips. He sends a strong electrical charge through them, even kicks them, but there's not a flicker of movement. The warm sheet of sandpaper passes over his face and crawls over his teeth and gums. He is clearly trapped inside his head, and his only option now is to wait for death. He hears the tinkle of bells apparently immersed in grease. Anxious, clumsy foot-steps approach. Someone has found his body and will perhaps bury it. However horrible his agony, at least the dogs won't eat him. Death begins with a grubby gnawing at the fingers. They either bite them off or chew, them in situ, before moving on to the palms of the hands. The tips of tongues clean out the gaps between the thick tendons of the thumb. The crunching of the radius sounds like the gentle crackle of a bony firework display. The shattered bones hang from the dangling sinews of the muscles. There is no pain at any point; it is all simply a matter of waiting, either angrily or patiently, for the teeth to reach the centres of power. Whether death comes from an infectious bite or a torn ventricle is of no importance. All that matters is his inability to raise his body and, with his only half-eaten hands, stop that orgy of dogs and microbes. Something shakes his face. A hand perhaps. Then a blow. The child inside the child trembles, holding onto his seat. In the midst of this internal earthquake, he unwittingly activates some hidden mechanism and manages to prise the other child's eyes open. The face of the goatherd, only inches from his, interposes itself like a lunar eclipse between him and the sun.

'Wake up, boy, wake up!'

⋆   ⋆   ⋆

The dog was licking one of the boy's hands as abrasively as it had previously been moistening his face and gums. The old man's sour breath burned the boy's newly opened eyes. He stammered out some incoherent comment as his gaze fixed on the goatherd's forehead, or more precisely on a pimple placed like a boundary post between his eyebrows. The man's face was dripping with sweat, and some drops slid down his nose, running over his skin like someone else's tears. He went to fetch something from one of the panniers on the donkey, then returned to where the boy was lying and knelt down beside him with a tin in his hand. He didn't need to open the boy's mouth because the sun had left the skin so tight that his mouth was like a buttonhole cut out of stiff leather. As tight as the skin of a suckling pig fresh from the oven. The goatherd took the precaution of administering the water by placing the edge of the mug on one corner of the boy's mouth, but the dog, circling inquisitively, distracted him for a moment and caused him inadvertently to tilt the tin so that the water poured straight down the child's throat. The boy choked and sat bolt upright like a crazed Lazarus. His absent gaze was still lost somewhere in his nightmare and, for a moment, he seemed barely human. The goatherd removed the tin and stood to one side as if fearing an imminent explosion. The glow of the sunset was slowly transforming reality, edging everything in red. The boy shattered the air with the cry of someone returning back down the tunnel that connects life and death. The old man heard that cry and, fortunately, was the only one to hear that broken voice crying in the wilderness.

In between giving the boy sips of water, with night fast closing in on them, the old man briefly reconnoitred the area round about and soon returned with a bunch of herbs and an abandoned honeycomb. He made a fire among the rocks, poured some oil into a blackened frying pan and quickly fried some plantain and calendula leaves. The strange odours from the leaves mingled with the medley of other aromas emanating from the animals and from that dark, drought-stricken plain. Hints of liquorice, oregano and cistus. Dried earth. Memories of the captive fig tree. Excrement and urine from the goats, sour cheese and the damp, warm stink of a fresh lump of dung deposited by the donkey a few feet away. The old man crumbled pieces of wax from the honeycomb into the hot mixture of fried leaves and, when he had mixed it all together, he spread the concoction onto strips of dirty rag. Lying next to the palm tree, the boy, partly out of weakness and partly out of necessity, uncomplainingly allowed the old man to wrap his head in these rags.

When the old man had finished, he arranged his blanket on the ground a few feet from where the boy was sitting and indicated that he should lie down on it. The boy got up and swayed slowly over to the blanket, like a reed with a very plump thrush perched on top. The man had provided him with the packsaddle as a pillow. The boy carefully laid his head down and made himself as comfortable as he could on the threadbare woollen blanket. From there, he perused the Milky Way from end to end as he listened to the old man coming and going and to the goats moving about nearby. That brilliant, peaceful band of stars. He identified the constellations he knew and, once again, followed the edge of the Plough that pointed to the North Star, He wondered if he would continue to walk in that direction when he recovered. He felt the stiff poultices cooling on his face, a mask in which the old man had left openings only for eyes and mouth. The damp, waxy cloth had not yet permeated through to his skin, which still felt horribly tight. He thought about what had happened, about this initial misfortune, which, right at the very outset, had left him lying prostrate on a blanket belonging to an old goatherd.

The smell of baking bread wafted past his face, and he noticed his mouth filling with saliva. He searched for the origin of that smell and saw the old man stamping out the small fire and scattering earth over it to douse the embers. Then the man walked over to him and stood at his feet. In the middle of the night, he seemed uncertain whether the boy would be awake or asleep. He jiggled the boy's leg with the tip of his boot, and before the boy had even moved, said:

'Food's ready.'

'Yes, sir.'

'Don't call me 'sir'.'

When the boy reached the spot where the fire had been, the old man was already eating, dunking bits of unleavened bread in a mug of wine. On a stone on the other side of the ashes stood an olive-wood bowl from which threads of steam were rising. The boy glanced at the man as if asking permission to enter his house, and with a lift of his chin, the old man indicated the bowl of fresh goat's milk. The boy sat down on the stone and raised the bowl to his lips. Some of the milk ran down the waxy folds of the poultice. The boy noticed that the tension around his mouth was easing slightly and that he could now shape his lips to the bowl. For a while, he merely took tiny sips, studying the old man out of the corner of his eye, so that he could easily avert his gaze if the man noticed him watching. The goatherd, however, was too absorbed in his own supper and paid no attention. At one point, the boy noticed that half the loaf the goatherd had baked was still there in the pan. He assumed the old man had left it for him, but didn't dare reach forward and pick it up. He made as if to get to his feet, but immediately fell back, gripped by embarrassment or fear.

'Go on, eat it.'

The boy softened the bread in his warm milk just as he had seen the goatherd do. He found it hard to chew and swallow but, in the circumstances, hunger overcame pain, as it always would from then on. While he was wiping the bowl clean with his bread, he realised that this was the first time he'd eaten anything hot since leaving home two nights before, and that it was the second time in only a few hours that he had eaten in the company of a stranger. Still holding the bowl, he realised that he had failed to foresee such basic contingencies as a lack of food or just how he would survive alone on that arid plain. He had left no room in his calculations for perhaps having to ask for help, far less at such an early stage in his journey. The truth was, he hadn't really prepared for his departure at all. One day, he had simply reached a point of no return and, from that moment on, the idea of running away became a necessary illusion that helped him with-stand the inferno of silence in which he was living. An idea that began to form in his mind as soon as his brain was ready for it and which then never left him. Apart from taking the knapsack with him and planning his escape on a moonless night, he had made no other real preparations or calculations. He had merely trusted in his knowledge and skills to help him on his way. After all, he was as much a child of that place as were the partridges or the olive trees. During the nights preceding his departure, while his brother slept by his side, he imagined himself laying traps for rabbits at the exits to their burrows or hunting quail with his catapult. He knew how to train ferrets; indeed, he had gone ferreting with his father ever since he was of an age to do so. They used to scout around for a bank or a sunken path full of burrows and cover each exit hole with a net held in place with wooden stakes. Then they would slip the ferret under one of the nets and wait. It took only a few seconds for the ferret to reach the spot where the rabbit was hiding, and one bite was enough to send the rabbit shooting out of one of the exits and straight into a net, which would close around it like a bag.

Then, sitting beneath the stars in the gentle night breeze, he would skewer his prey and roast it over a fire like the one the goatherd had lit. It hadn't occurred to him that he would need water or where he would find it. He hadn't planned out an itinerary. His mental map ended at the edge of the olive grove to the north of the village and beyond which he knew nothing. He had imagined that, behind the hills, he would find infinite olive groves and that it would simply be a matter of going from trunk to trunk, from shade to shade, until he found a better place to live. However, beyond the last olive tree lay the plain, in the midst of which he now found himself. He didn't know how far exactly he was from the village, and the only people who could tell him were either still pursuing him or, like the old man, barely spoke.

The goatherd rounded off his meal by gnawing on a wedge of hard cheese, then, when he'd finished, got up, walked over to the boy, cut another wedge of cheese and, without even looking at him, held it out. The boy took it and immediately started gnawing on it too. The old man turned then and, walking round the now extinguished fire, spread the blanket from the donkey on the ground. From the pannier, he took a couple of yellowing strips of dried cod. He scraped off as much salt as he could and placed the fish in a bowl, which he filled with water. Then, as if he were entirely alone in the world, he farted a couple of times and prepared for bed. The boy noticed that the goatherd had difficulty in bending down and in accommodating his bony body among the stones.

The boy remained sitting on the stone for a long time after he had finished his supper. It was as if he had once again entered a house full of rules and was waiting for someone to issue an order or give him permission before he could go to bed. On the other side of the fire, the old man's snores mingled with the whirring of the cicadas and the crickets. High up, the breeze set the fronds of the palm tree dancing, and the boy watched them swaying above the accumulation of dead foliage hanging from the trunk. He lifted one finger in search of a breeze he could not find. Up there, he thought, the air would be purer than the air near the ground and he thought, too, that the palm tree must have done something to deserve that balmy air. He touched the waxy mask on his face, and his skin felt warmer and softer. He must have done something to deserve his burns, his hunger and his family. 'Something bad,' as his father never tired of telling him.

The dog woke him up at daybreak, prodding his neck with its moist nose. The poultice had come off during the night and now lay in a stinking heap next to his head. He touched his face and noticed a couple of blisters on his cheekbones. His skin felt less tight than it had the day before, but was still quite stiff. The goatherd was sitting in the same spot where he had eaten his supper, chewing now on a piece of dried cod, from which a whitish liquid dripped, and taking long draughts of wine from a wineskin. The boy sat up on the blanket and tried to catch the goatherd's eye, but the old man paid no attention. Beside him, the bowl he had emptied the night before was now full of fresh milk thickened with oats. He picked up the bowl and the wood felt warm in his hands. He again sought the goatherd's eyes, and although he knew his gaze would not be returned, he raised the bowl to him as a sign of gratitude.

During breakfast, he witnessed, for the first time, the harnessing of the donkey, a liturgy that he himself would go on to perform for the rest of his days and which, in time, would become part of a larger ritual, that of his profession and of a life spent constantly on the move.

The old man grabbed the donkey's halter and pulled the animal to its feet. Without unhobbling it, he placed on its back a large canvas saddle pad. On top of this, he added a worn hessian cloth and then a packsaddle stuffed with rye straw and a breeching strap that went around the haunches. Before loading the donkey he redistributed the straw stuffing, which, during the previous day's journey, had migrated to the lower parts of the saddle, then he secured it all with a thick esparto-grass cinch strap that went under the donkey's belly. He spread a blanket over the packsaddle, an action that reminded the boy of the moment in mass when the priest turned back to the altar after celebrating communion and, with the help of the altar boy, placed on top of the chalice the corporal-cloth, the paten, the purifier and the key to the sacrarium.

Finally, on top of everything else, the old man placed four esparto panniers attached to a frame, with two panniers on either side. The donkey, which had been perfectly placid until then, made as if to set off. The old man soothed it by stroking its muzzle and running his fingers through the tuft of hair between the donkey's ears.

The goatherd then shared out the load among the four panniers, and when all his belongings were safely stowed away, reviewed the situation and gave a sigh. He repositioned a few smaller objects, secured the trivet and the frying pan more firmly, and only then did he remove the rope hobble tethering the donkey's two front legs.

The dog was scampering about, herding the goats up so close to the donkey's hind legs that the donkey occasionally tried to kick them out of the way. The old man surveyed the campsite and counted the goats, pointing to each of them in turn. He then put on his hat and held out one hand to the boy.

'The blanket.'

The boy sprang to his feet, picked up the blanket and gave it to him. The old man took it and used it to cover the contents of the panniers. He then whistled to the dog and, as on the first occasion they had met, the dog raced over to the stray goats and herded them together, barking and snapping. The boy wondered if his own day would also be a repetition of the previous one: an early breakfast followed by a long walk in the blazing sun. The old man grabbed the halter and tugged at it twice. The donkey set off after him, panniers swaying, and the rest of his retinue followed behind. The boy stayed where he was, watching the flock pass slowly by, with its usual cacophony of bleating and clanking of bells seemingly tuned to every possible register. The old man and the donkey were at the front, the dog chasing madly after them, and last of all came the goats, leaving behind a slipstream of dung like the tail of a comet. When they had gone about twenty yards, the old man stopped and turned round:

'Come on, I can't wait for you all day.'

4

They walked for a couple of hours over unploughed fields, with the boy keeping close to the donkey, as the old man had told him to. They paused in one field where there were still the remains of the last harvest. The goats immediately scattered and, heads down, began nibbling the stubble. The boy, who had covered his head with his shirt, observed the scene from the shade afforded him by the donkey. The old man remained standing, surveying the vast space surrounding them. Shading his eyes with his hand, he paused for a moment, gazing towards the south. Then he took his tobacco pouch out of his bag and rolled himself a cigarette. When he had finished, he gazed up at the clear sky and scanned it from side to side. He took off his hat to cool his head, whistled to the dog, and off they went.

They crossed the stony ground at such a slow pace that they didn't even kick up any dust. The landscape they passed through, full of abandoned arable fields and threshing floors, spoke to them of desolation. As did the flattened furrows covered in a crust of baked earth so hard that it only gave beneath the hooves of the heavily laden donkey. Fields as corrugated as washboards and sown with waxy, sharp-edged flints thrown up by the threshers. There came a point when the sun was so high that the donkey was no longer protecting the boy with its shade, and he kept trying to arrange his shirt so that it covered both head and shoulders. He occasionally glanced at the old man, trying to communicate his distress, but the old man, impervious to the heat, continued on in the same direction, as if they were strolling along the shore of a mountain lake. Once, the boy hung back to rearrange his turban. The dog stayed by him, wagging its tail and running around him as if his master's companion were a new toy. In order to adjust the shirt to his head, the boy flailed around with his arms, snorting angrily, as if this would somehow help to make the shirt bigger or oblige the old man to find a shady beech wood in the middle of nowhere. At best, all he managed was to get the goatherd to stop, not in order to wait for him, but to pretend to be pouring water out of an empty flask. Seeing the man ahead of him raising the mug to his lips, the boy stopped fiddling with his shirt-cum-turban and hurried on in order to reach the old man before all the water was gone. When he got there, with his shirt draped haphazardly over his head, the old man was already putting the cork back in the flask. He would then whistle to the dog and carry on walking.

Finally, when the sun's heat had become unbearable, they stopped. A few yards away from a reed bed, on the edge of what must once have been a pond, stood two exhausted alder trees, their leaves all shrivelled. Along one side, beyond the main clump of reeds, grew a thin line of pale, parched foliage, like a barb piercing the plain. On the other side, lines like isobars were etched on the dry, cracked bed of the pond, witnesses to its final death throes, grubby traces left by the water and which the process of evaporation had imprinted on the now dry mud. The hot midday breeze made the reeds rustle, filling the air with a sound like delicate wooden bells. Coarse heads of hair waving like Tibetan prayer flags, albeit unadorned by spirited horses, jewels or mantras. Cries addressed to the heavens which, instead of bestowing blessings, seemed to call upon the sun to bring down still more fire with the help of a piece of glass or a lightning bolt.

The goatherd led the donkey over to the alder trees and there began to unload it. The boy watched him absently, driven almost mad by thirst or perhaps by their sudden arrival at a resting-place he had lost all hope of finding. The pustules on his face had grown redder. The old man turned to him, his hands resting lightly on the donkey's rope bridle. The boy, covered in dust, stood there petrified.

'Boy.'

The goatherd's voice dragged him back out of the abyss into which he had fallen and, almost without realising it, he turned towards that voice. The old man had stopped what he was doing and was, for the first time, looking him in the face. He was squinting in the bright light, his eyes shaded by the two bony arches protecting his milky corneas. The old man's penetrating gaze restored him to normality, like a surgeon setting a fracture with one precise, decisive movement.

'Boy.'

The second time the old man spoke, the boy sprang into action and went to his aid. He took the various objects the old man passed to him and placed them under the trees. When they had unloaded the donkey, the man took one of the flasks and plunged into the reed bed, pushing the reeds and bulrushes aside with his hands. The boy watched him disappear and saw how the goats followed down the path he had opened up. Then he uncorked the flask left in one of the panniers and tipped it into his tin. Not a

61

drop. He looked over at the gap in the reeds into which the goatherd had vanished and, squeezing the tin hard in his hands, he cursed him roundly.

He sat down and leaned his back against the trunk of one of the trees and studied the landscape. He thought of the *reguera*, the stream into which the village poured its sewage. He remembered how it stank, remembered the clumps of bulrushes, the ailanthus trees and the reeds growing along its banks. He regarded the pale little copse of alders as if it were a fossil, then stood up and walked along the edge of the reed bed. The dog remained where it was, lying in the feeble shade provided by the trees. Walking over the surface of the absent water, he felt an unconscious impulse to roll up his trouser legs so as not to get them wet, a desire for cool, clean water that was felt, rather, by his cells, with their different way of perceiving reality. He found signs of moisture at the foot of a willow. A multitude of tiny channels, like a miniature delta, flowing towards the now absent pond. An attempt that led off beyond the shade cast by the reeds only to be frustrated by the sun and the rain-starved earth. A pointless exercise inscribed on the soft, sandy sediment.

When he got back to the encampment, the

old man had already sorted out the goats, who, crammed together among the reeds, only stayed there for a while, their noses in the mud, until the old man felt they'd had enough to drink and shooed them out, slapping them on the back. Like a shoal of fish, other goats immediately filled any vacant spaces. When the goatherd saw the boy return, he pointed to the alder tree where the donkey was grazing. Next to it were two flasks. The boy went over and shook them. Then he uncorked one, filled his tin with water and drank. The water tasted muddy. He could feel the grit in his throat and between his teeth, but he didn't care.

They ate, sitting leaning against the tree trunks, surrounded by the goats, the donkey and the dog, who all crowded in under the trees as if, beyond the shade, lay a deep abyss. When they had finished eating, the old man got up and moved a few yards off to urinate, his back turned to the camp. He didn't return immediately and, from his place in the shade, the boy saw him bend down and fiddle with something on the ground. He thought he must be tying the lace on one of his boots. The old man returned, however, carrying a thick aloe leaf. He sat down in the spot where they'd eaten and, with a penknife, peeled the skin off the broad base of the leaf and handed it to the boy so that he could apply it to the burns on his face.

They spent the siesta hours beneath the trees, the boy smearing his burns with the transparent jelly from the aloe leaf and the goatherd carving a new wooden hook for the donkey's cinch strap. Later on, when the sun had lost some of its heat, the old man picked up a sickle and asked the boy to follow him over to a clump of esparto grass growing on the far side of the pond. Before they reached it, though, the boy felt uneasy and stopped. The old man turned, expecting to find the boy behind him. Then, with the sickle in one hand, he beckoned him over. The boy, standing some way off, shook his head. The man shouted:

'Watch me.'

He crouched down in front of a clump of grass and with two short blows cut off a thick tuft. He held it up so that the boy could see, then put it down at his feet along with the sickle. The goatherd then went back to the camp, and when he passed the boy, told him to make eight or ten bundles of grass and take them over to the alder trees. The boy turned and waited until the old man had disappeared again behind the bulrushes. Then he walked over to the sickle and for a moment contemplated the countryside around him: the little islands of scrub and the stony paths that ran between them. He went hunting for the largest clumps of grass, and when he found what he wanted, set to work. He hadn't said anything to the goatherd when the latter had shown him how to cut the grass, but this was a job he knew how to do well because, at home, he had always been the one who kept the ground around the house cleared.

The boy concluded his labours as evening was coming on. He gathered up the grass and started carrying it in bundles over to the shade. He left the first bundle next to the goatherd and went back for more. The old man, who was milking a goat, briefly stopped what he was doing, then immediately resumed his work. No thanks, no reward. The law of the plain.

They dined on bread and milk and, afterwards, the boy applied more aloe jelly to his face. He fell asleep watching the goatherd making ropes by plaiting the grass he had cut that afternoon. He didn't even hear the distant sound of hooves crossing the dark plain. Nor did he see how the goatherd's hand trembled, startled by this sudden noise cleaving through the arid plain like a stone sword. The only thing he felt, when the time came, was the old man's boot prodding him in the back and his voice telling him to get up.

He did as he was told, thinking that it must be dawn already and that the goatherd would again have prepared his breakfast for him. He felt around him for the bowl, but the only thing he found was the blanket he had slept on. Everything else, including the bundles of grass, was already loaded onto the donkey.

'Pick up the blanket. We're leaving.'

* * *

The crescent moon was still only a yellow sliver on the horizon. The old man tugged at the donkey's bridle and strode off, with the herd following behind. The dog came and went in the darkness, retrieving any stray goats. Clinging to the donkey's halter, the boy stumbled after them. When they left the encampment in the middle of the night, the boy had assumed they were leaving before dawn in order to avoid the crushing noonday sun. To judge by the route followed on the previous days, the boy had assumed that the old man knew the region well and would again stop at midday beside some copse or stream. But as time passed and the darkness failed to lift and the pace at which they were walking remained undiminished, he realised that they were no longer in pursuit of pastures new.

At dawn, they stopped at the foot of a sun-scorched hill, whose top concealed the horizon. The goatherd let go of the bridle and walked on ahead for a few yards. He went first in one direction then in the other, raising and lowering his head as if searching for something among the shadows. He rubbed his face with his hands and massaged his eyelids with the tips of his fingers, all the while huffing and puffing. He closed his eyes and raised his face to the sky to breathe in the faint breeze coming down from the hill. He sniffed at the invisible door opening before him until he found, among all the other smells of daybreak, the thread that had brought them there.

Seeing that they were stopping for rather longer than expected, the boy sat down on the ground to rest. He felt the weight of his body seeking the earth. He would have lain down and slept right there on the baked clay, but a foul-smelling breeze brought him to his senses. He stood up just as the goatherd came striding back, The old man glanced behind him, checked that the herd were all there, then set off again. They climbed up the slope, weaving in and out of long-since withered vines. The wild tendrils twined about each other, weaving a futile, fossil web.

When they reached the top, the horizon

reappeared. Beyond, the plateau plunged downwards to form a valley from which there emanated, even more strongly, the same stench he had noticed at the foot of the hill. The boy tried to identify where the smell was coming from, but there was still not enough light at that hour to be able to make out the coral-like shapes of the bone pit that lay beneath them.

They descended via a narrow track, trying to keep the donkey from slipping. The goats made the descent as best they could, scattering shards of slate, which skittered down to the bottom of the abyss. Axes fracturing gleaming white ribs. Bones in every possible state of degradation. Sediments of calcic dust, rows of bovine vertebrae, broad pelvises. Ribcages and horns. An eyeless animal, its skin still intact. A stinking bag of bones in the midst of the new day dawning. A lighthouse guiding them to a safe harbour.

★　★　★

They set up camp some distance from the putrefying ox, in the arching shade of a hawthorn. The goats dispersed among the bones in search of grass, and only the donkey, the dog, the boy and the man remained, like figures in a nativity scene. They breakfasted

68

on bread dipped in wine and lay down to rest. The boy fell asleep almost instantly, with a feeling that his muscles were softening and melding inside his body. Before he succumbed to unconsciousness, his final thoughts were of the sleepless night he'd spent, the drowsiness brought on by the wine, his filthy hands and the pestilential, walled-in pit surrounding him.

When he woke, the old man was no longer by his side. He climbed up out of the crater and saw the goatherd kneeling on the highest edge. He was looking south, shading his eyes with both hands, as if he were wearing spectacles. The boy watched as he made his way gingerly back down the stony slope, half-crouching, half-sitting, so as not to slip. Some of the goats had lain down in the shade and others, unobstructed for the moment by any human presence, were standing on their back legs to reach the higher branches of the hawthorn.

The boy wandered about in the shade to stretch his legs and discovered that, while he slept, the old man had plaited most of the esparto grass into ropes. He squatted down and tested the strength of the ropes and wondered what the old man could possibly want with so much of the stuff. The goatherd returned from his patrol and, without a word, sat down under the hawthorn tree again to continue his work, The boy said he was going for a walk.

'Don't go far.'

'I won't.'

He had never seen a place like this before. There were skulls everywhere. Hollow, broken bones like the stems of giant fennel. The worn teeth of ruminants. Noticing the billy goat searching for food near the dead ox, he went over to join it. When he reached its side, however, the goat started and accidentally struck the body with its horns, causing a rat that had been hiding inside to peep out. The rat hid under the ox's pelvis, nervously sniffed the air, then returned to its feeding trough. When the boy rejoined the old man, he told him what he had seen. The man stopped what he was doing, got to his feet and, taking a stick and a blanket, went over to where the ox lay rotting. The boy followed him to within a few yards of the cadaver. For a while, they crouched there in silence, observing the rippling movements of the skin. A crow alighted on the creature's side. The skin undulated over the ribs like the softened hull of a ship. The animal had been emptied of its contents and was now a mere façade with only one opening where the genitals had been. The goatherd got up and walked in a silent arc round to the animal's head. The crow flapped away. The boy watched the old man cover nose and mouth with one arm before walking the length of the corpse to its rear end, using the blanket to cover the one opening in the animal's hide. Then he stamped on the ribs with his boot and the rat immediately scampered out of its cave and into the trap. The old man beat the woollen blanket until the rat stopped moving.

By evening, the goatherd had made some netting out of the esparto grass. He found four stout branches, cleaned them off and with the branches and the netting fashioned a small corral, into which, with the help of the dog, he herded the goats. Once they were all inside, he gave each of them some water to drink from a bowl. When they had finished, only a third of a flask of water was left. The boy asked the old man about this, and the old man told him not to worry. That night they would drink milk, and the following day they would set off in search of a new spring.

Afterwards, the goatherd went to fetch a stool and placed it next to the one corner of the corral that could be opened. He fixed the bucket in the ground with the metal rods and turned to the boy.

'You're going to help me milk the goats.'

'But I've never done it before.'

'You just stand at the gate of the corral and

let the goats out one by one when I tell you to.'

They finished milking in a matter of minutes, and the boy was surprised at how little milk the goats had given. The old man explained that at this time of year, what with the heat, and the lack of water or any pasture worthy of the name, the goats didn't have much milk to give.

When night fell, the old man skinned the rat, splayed its body out on a cross made of twigs, and lit a small fire. The boy didn't want to eat the rat, and so the goatherd shared it with the dog. There were still a few almonds and raisins in a small basket, but the old man didn't offer him any and the boy didn't ask.

5

The old man woke the boy in the middle of the night. They left the bone pit the same way they had entered, then circled around it before setting off towards the north. Unlike the previous day, the boy felt rested and more reassured about what lay ahead. They crossed the plain beneath a moon that was not yet bright enough to light the ground they walked on. As the boy clung to the donkey's halter, the animal's swaying gait seemed to him like a litany as monotonous as the landscape they were crossing. Dark sky, dark horizon and dark, desolate fields. Guided by the old man and supported by the donkey, he abandoned himself to memories of the place he had come from. His village was perched above a river bed, where water had once flowed, but which was now just a long, broad indentation in the midst of an interminable plain. Most of the houses, many of them empty, were built around the church and the medieval palace. Beyond them, like a belt of asteroids, lay a scattering of crumbling walls, all that remained of the fields that had once fed the village. The streets were flanked by houses with whitewashed roughcast walls and gable roofs, with crudely made grilles at the windows and metal doors concealed behind curtains. The gates on yards were kept firmly shut to protect the wooden carts and threshing machines. There was a time when the plain had been an ocean of wheatfields and, on windy spring days, the ears of wheat rippled just like the surface of the sea. Fragrant green waves waiting for the summer sun. The same sun that now fermented the clay and ground it down into dust.

He remembered the fringe of olive trees that extended along the north side of the river bed. The very olive grove in which he had taken refuge. An ancient, woody army tingeing the landscape with leathery browns. Often, each tree was supported by two or three gnarled trunks that reached up out of the earth like an old man's arthritic fingers. It was rare to see an olive tree that really looked like a tree. Instead, there were endless knotty trunks full of deep cracks into which the rain had first penetrated, then frozen and split the wood open. A bunch of soldiers returned from the front. Wounded, but still marching. A march that had been going on for so long that no one could now testify as to their continued advance. They were not witnesses of the passage of time, but rather time owed its very nature to them.

He mentally travelled along the railway line that traversed the village from east to west, following the axis of the old valley. It arrived raised up on embankments and sleepers and disappeared into the distance as if scissored out of the landscape. On one side was the village proper, with the church, the town hall, the barracks and the palace. On the other, a group of low houses built around an abandoned vinegar factory. The vaulted roofs on some of the warehouses had caved in and a pestilential smell percolated out from a rusty tank, little by little, day by day, like an unending curse. The time spent in the bone pit seemed positively pleasant in comparison with the invisible atmosphere generated by that place. Next to the factory, the single railway track branched off into three. Beside it stood the station building with its cantilevered roof and broken windows. In the centre was a platform like a large island lit by half a dozen rather feeble gas lamps and, next to this, a brick-built cattle-loading yard and two sheds with doors barred shut. Beyond that, above the last set of tracks, rose a faded-yellow grain silo crowned by a red sign bearing the word 'ELECTRA'. A vast, imposing edifice that dwarfed everything else, and from whose roof one could see the mountains to the north marking the end of the plateau. A great hulk casting a dark, oppressive shadow.

His family lived in one of the village's few stone houses. It had been built by the railway company at one end of the station, just where the line was crossed by the road leading towards the fields to the south. Everyone called it the pointsman's house. On summer evenings, the shadow cast by the silo completely covered the roof and part of the surrounding yard — an area of trampled earth that was home to a dozen or so hens and three piglets. Apart from the bailiff and the priest, no one else in the village kept animals.

Before the drought, his father had been in charge of the crossing-gate and had helped the stationmaster with the points. Four times a day he would work the mechanism that lowered the gate with one hand, while ringing a bell with the other. A few truck drivers would turn off their engines, get out and roll themselves a cigarette while they watched the slow convoys heading off in the direction of the sea. Those were the days when the trucks would arrive empty and leave laden with oats, wheat and barley from the silo. Then the drought came, and the fields gradually languished, then died. The grain stopped growing, and the railway company either scrapped the wagons or simply abandoned them. They closed down the station and despatched the stationmaster somewhere further east. In one year, more than half the families in the village left. Those who survived were the few who had deep wells or had made money out of the cereal crops and others who had neither well nor money, but submitted themselves to the new rules imposed by that drought-stricken land. His family belonged to the latter category and stayed on.

*   *   *

They stopped to rest near some old almond trees. It was a warm night, and they drank nearly all of the little water they had left. It seemed to the boy that, this time, the goatherd knew where they were going. At one point, they reached a wire fence and followed it until they came to an opening through which they passed over to the other side. They crossed a barren field that emerged onto a new path heading west. This sudden change of direction away from the north made the boy think that perhaps the goatherd still had no fixed destination and was merely wandering aimlessly. As long as they kept moving away from the village, that was all the boy cared about.

At first light, they spotted the remains of a large building on the horizon. The undulating ground meant that, as they advanced, the ruin appeared and disappeared behind the withered crops. As they climbed the last steep slope, the details of this elusive edifice were gradually revealed: a high stone-and-mortar wall topped by crenellated battlements and separated from the path by stony ground. This solitary wall, marked by several putlock holes, survived only thanks to the round tower to which it was attached. On top of the tower someone had placed a figure of Jesus holding up his hand to bless the plain. From behind his head emerged three bronze rays of lights. The boy recognised the image and immediately recalled the legend that all the children in the village would have heard at one time or another. According to the most common version, a castle had been built to the north or north-east of the village. It was inhabited by a man who, apart from his fearsome guards, lived entirely alone. This man spent his days and nights standing on the wall with one hand raised, warning travellers not to approach. Others said that he wasn't raising his hand, but wielding a weapon, while still others said that from his head emanated rays of light that swept the plain in all directions. There was also talk of wild dogs and of how the guards would capture children and take them to the man so that he could inflict the most savage tortures on them.

They descended via a gentle slope leading down to the castle and stopped midway to take a closer look. The path continued on a little to join a towpath that ran parallel to an old aqueduct, whose broken pillars shimmered in the hot air rising up from the earth. They could still see the vast ravine along which barges had once travelled, laden with timber and sacks of wheat. They left the path and crossed the area of stony ground, stopping, either out of caution or unconscious fear, at a point where they would not be crushed were the wall to collapse. For a long time, they stood contemplating the ruins, as if they were some rare marvel: the wall, the round tower to the left and, beyond that, the horizon from which they had come. To one side of the tower was a rounded arch containing a bricked-up door. On the highest part of the wall, above the keystone of the arch, was a machicolation supported by three corbels. For their part, the goats happily dispersed, guided only by their need for food in the form of dry tufts of grass. If the wall did collapse, it would kill almost all of them. The boy paused to examine the sculpture, which reminded him of the image of the Sacred Heart of Jesus in the village church. Just for a moment, he felt a desire to go back and rejoin the other children in the school playground and tell them about his discovery and tell them, above all, that there was no need to visit a castle in order to be terrified, that terror rode the streets of the village in the form of a backfiring motorbike and clouds of toxic smoke.

After a while, the boy turned to the old man, expecting him to abandon his contemplation in order to unload the donkey and to rest. However, the old man continued to stand there, staring blankly at the wall. The boy thought he must have gone to sleep. From his lesser height, he could see the old man's wide nostrils and the long white hairs sprouting from the darkness within; his grizzled four days' growth of beard; and his jaw from which hung the slack skin of his blank face. The boy felt like tugging at his sleeve and dragging him away, but could not allow himself such familiarity. He cleared his throat, scratched the back of his neck and shifted from foot to foot like someone desperate for a pee, but still he couldn't get the old man's attention.

'Sir.'

The goatherd spun round as if he'd been insulted, and only then did they start to walk towards the wall. When they reached it, the old man almost collapsed against it, and it was the boy who took charge of unloading the donkey. He removed the various bits and pieces from the panniers on the pack frame and placed them next to the old man. When he'd finished doing this, he detached the panniers themselves and put the goatherd's belongings back inside them. The old man asked him to bring him the packsaddle to use as a pillow. The boy tried to get it off the donkey by lifting it from the side, but it was too well embedded on the animal's back and, however hard he tried, he couldn't shift it. He searched the panniers for a length of rope left over from the netting and tied it to the donkey's cinch strap. Then he attached the other end to a large piece of stone fallen from the castle wall and gave a tug on the halter. The donkey immediately started forward, and the saddle slipped backwards over its rump onto the ground.

He carried the packsaddle over to the goatherd and, seeing him from close to, the boy thought that not only did he look much tireder than on previous days, he looked quite ill. The old man said that they would stay there for a couple of days because there was a well nearby, plus it was the only shade they would find for many miles and there was food for the goats. The boy glanced around him and, for as far as he could see, there was nothing but stones and baked earth. The only food available for the goats was a few withered clumps of astragalus and some scattered stubble left from the last harvest. Up until then, they had always managed to find shade and, as regards food for the goats, this was one of the poorest places they had camped. He turned to the old man and found him lying down on the stones, his head resting on the pack-saddle and his hat covering his face. The boy assumed that he must be exhausted after so much walking and that they had stopped there because the man could go no further. He bent down and, picking up the flasks, shook them to see how much water they had left.

★   ★   ★

At midday, the boy managed to load the panniers onto the donkey's back and in them placed the flasks and the milking pail. From where he lay, the goatherd described exactly what he would find, pointed him in the direction he should take and, before he left, lent him his straw hat.

Although the water tank was right next to the well and was clearly visible from the castle, by the time the boy reached it, sweat was pouring down his face. There was the water tank, just as the old man had said and, a few yards away, the well itself with a brick arch from which hung a four-pointed hook. Someone had thrown sticks down the shaft, making it impossible to lower the bucket into the water. With the help of the hook, however, he managed to remove some of the sticks and make a gap large enough for the bucket to pass through.

It took him a couple of hours to fill the two flasks. He put in the corks, but when he tried to pick up the first one to carry it over to the donkey, it was far too heavy. He had to empty out half the water from each flask, and even then it was a titanic struggle to lift them into the panniers.

He returned to the castle in the late afternoon, exhausted by his efforts. The old man was lying where he had left him hours before. The boy unloaded the water, removed the panniers and hobbled the donkey. Then, when he'd finished giving water to the goats, he sat down next to the old man and stayed there, watching the light change in texture as the sun set behind the wall. He heard pigeons cooing as they returned to the tower to roost.

By the light of the half-moon they dined on rancid almonds and raisins and when they had finished, the boy tidied up, then cleared the stones away from a spot a couple of yards from where the old man was lying. In doing so, he discovered the delicate, smiling skull of a hare. He held it in his hands and ran his fingertips over its complex contours. He imagined its head fixed on a small oval of dark wood, as if it were a miniature hunting trophy. The brass plaque underneath would bear the name of the hunter and the date on which he had felled the beast. He put the skull to one side, rolled up the saddle-cloth and placed it under his head. He was so tired that even the smell of donkey exuded by this makeshift pillow seemed almost pleasant. He said goodnight to the old man and, as usual, received no reply. Lying down, he scanned the heavens in search of the constellations he knew, then turned his attention to the moon. Its milky glow hurt his retinas. He closed his eyes and, from behind his lids, he could still see that arc of dazzling light. He remembered the skull he had found while he was preparing his bed. Memories of the bailiff's gallery of hunting trophies paraded past beneath his moist eyelids. He recalled the first time he'd entered that place. His father had gone with him. The acrid smell of wood and the creaking floorboards, the like of which he had never seen before. The two of them waiting in the gloomy reception room, with his father clutching his hat to his chest, obsessively turning it round and round. The dark coffered ceiling and the vast room adorned with the heads of mouflon, deer and bulls.

'Is this your boy?'

'Yes, sir.'

'What a lovely child.'

The memory of the bailiff's voice pierced his eyes, and it was as if blood were springing up from beneath his swollen eyelids. Staring skywards, he bit his lips and felt a kind of oily liquid filling his tear ducts and blocking his nose. He sniffed hard, trying to clear his airways, and the noise he made alarmed him because he was afraid the goatherd might hear.

'Don't be afraid. Nothing bad's going to happen to you.'

The old man's voice seemed to emerge from the earth itself, cutting a path through the rocky strata in order to destroy the toxic cloud threatening to engulf him. The boy was struck dumb, his neck stiffened. Then, from somewhere, he heard the whirr of cicadas and began to swallow down his tears, until he felt pure air once more penetrating his nostrils. He dried his eyes, placed his two hands together beneath one cheek and, shortly afterwards, fell asleep.

Despite having lain down to sleep a couple of yards away from the goatherd, he woke the following morning to find himself lying pressed up against the old man's motionless body. The harsh glare from the plain forced open his eyes, and the first thing he noticed was the putrid smell emanating from the old man, as potent as the smell he himself gave off, only less familiar. He blinked in an attempt to wake himself up and crept back to the spot where he had originally lain down, hoping that the goatherd was still asleep. The old man, who had been lying in exactly the same position all night, turned his head and asked the boy to bring him a goat. The boy felt ashamed when he realised that the old man had woken before him and he was at a loss as to how he could interpret the fact that their two bodies had remained so close, and that the goatherd hadn't moved away. He stood up and brushed the dust off his clothes. His shirt was covered in large grease stains and the bottoms of his trousers hung in tatters.

After breakfast, the old man asked the boy to use the blanket to make an awning to protect him from the morning sun. The boy stuffed two corners of the blanket into holes in the wall, then propped up the rest of the blanket on two poles. When he had finished, he sat down next to the old man, albeit out of the shade, awaiting new instructions, because this was how their new life together was taking shape. The goatherd, constrained by the growing stiffness in his joints, taking shelter from the inclement sky. The boy, like an energetic extension of the old man, prepared for whatever labours the plain and the elements demanded of him. For some time, they remained quite still, the old man leaning back against the saddle and the boy waiting in the sun. When the boy could bear it no longer, he got up, walked round to the other side of the wall and lay down in the torrid shade beyond, where he fell asleep. The sun again woke him as it rose above the top of the wall. He returned to the goatherd's side and they ate a few bits of cheese and a little of the remaining dried meat.

The old man spent most of the afternoon reading an ancient Bible with rounded corners, which he kept wrapped in a piece of cloth. He followed the words with one finger, pronouncing them syllable by syllable. Meanwhile, the boy set off to explore the ruins with the dog. He was able to map the plan of the castle from what remained of the foundations and he wondered where all the stones from the walls and vaults had gone. He discovered a few desiccated lizards and some pellets full of fragments of bone and fur. On the south-east side of the wall he came across feathers and bits of twisted skin which he interpreted as the leftovers from some owl's banquet.

At the far end of the area opposite the wall, he scrambled down a bank full of rabbit-holes. The boy went back to where the old man was lying and told him about the tracks and droppings he had found. He also told him about his experiences of ferreting and how closely it resembled the way the old man had trapped the rat in the bone pit. He spoke of days spent hunting on the railway embankments and how, when he caught a rabbit, he would kill it by holding it by its back legs and striking it with a stick on the back of the neck. 'The rabbit goes like this,' he said, pulling a face and holding out trembling arms. According to the boy, July was the best month for catching partridge chicks. 'You have to go out at midday, when it's hottest, and if you find a female with her chicks, you choose one and run after it. It soon gets tired.' Then, without mentioning his mother, he described, as if they were his own, his techniques for skinning a rabbit and breaking the neck of a young pigeon. Beside him, the dog was wagging its tail as if wanting to breathe life into the boy's adventurous daydreams. When the boy had finished, the old man said there was no point in hunting rabbits, because in order to cook them they would have to make a fire and that could attract the men who were looking for him. The boy felt deflated by this negative response, because he had thought that, for once, he had something to offer that man who seemed to know everything. Indeed, he was so discouraged that he didn't even take in what the old man had just said to him.

They spent the rest of the day apart. The goatherd with his Bible and the boy with the dog on the other side of the wall. As darkness fell, the old man used his crook to get hold of the food pouch, from which he took out a crust of bread and the last of the rancid almonds. While he was waiting for the boy to return, he tried to crack open the almonds with two stones. His hands were trembling so much, though, that he couldn't get the shells in the right position. On one attempt he hit his own fingers and the pain made him snort with rage. When the sun had almost set, the boy returned to the old man's side. He was carrying a stick in one hand and a rabbit in the other. The dog was scampering around him.

Despite his aching bones, it was the old man who took charge of skinning the rabbit.

He weighed it in his hands and, for a moment, seemed very pleased with the specimen. Then he made a few cuts in the creature's legs and abdomen and pulled off the skin leaving the animal naked. He threw the innards to the dog, then asked the boy to help him to his feet. They went over to the tower and, while the old man was making a fireplace out of stones, the boy went in search of kindling. They roasted the rabbit just as they had the rat. They did not speak during supper, too busy gnawing every last scrap of meat off the bones. When they had finished, the old man rolled a cigarette and the boy took charge of dousing the fire and getting rid of the bones and skin. It was then, while he was burying the remains far from the castle, that he recalled what the old man had said about the dangers of lighting a fire. He completed his burial of the remains by scuffing up earth onto the grave with his boots, then he rejoined the goatherd. He found him standing with his back to him, a few yards away from his blanket, one hand resting on the wall while he urinated. The smoke from his cigarette wrapped about his head like a cloud of grey thoughts.

'How did you know that some men were looking for me?'

The old man stood as still and silent as

Lot's wife watching Sodom burn. The boy waited. Without removing his hand from the wall, the goatherd finished urinating and shook his penis dry. When he turned, the boy noticed that the man's trousers were wet and that the pink tip of his penis was protruding from his flies.

The boy fled into the night, his subconscious drawing him back to the place where he had buried the remains of the rabbit just minutes before. He stumbled on, skidding on the stones, running as fast as he could in the direction of the well. Then he caught his foot on the stop-cock next to the water tank and fell. He lay in the darkness feeling the blood throbbing in his foot. Once he had calmed down, he crept over to the water tank and sat there, his back against the brick surround. From where he was he had only a very partial view of the wall and the plain. The image of the old man turning clumsily towards him completely filled his thoughts. The moist tip of the goatherd's penis, the skinned rabbit, the search party. He assumed that this stopping-place was merely a kind of meeting-point where he would be handed over to the bailiff. The old man, he thought, had been pretending to be in pain and had led him to those ruins so that he could be safely executed far from the village. He imagined the goatherd sitting at the foot of the wall calmly witnessing his martyrdom. He wished himself far away, wished he had been better able to bear his fate. The sound of distant goat-bells distracted him and, for a while, he gazed up at the castle, but could see no activity, no movement. Later, when he had recovered from running at full pelt immediately after eating, he allowed himself to be lulled by the sound of the bells and fell asleep, sitting up, his head drooping over his chest.

Just before dawn, he was woken by the dog pressing its cold nose against his bent neck. Still half-asleep, the boy pushed it away, but the dog insisted. The boy opened his eyes and the first thing he saw was the dog wagging its tail. Round its neck was the tin the goatherd had given him the first time they had met. The boy stroked the dog, then yawned and stretched. He saw the rusty stopcock he had tripped over the night before and, still without removing his boot, tentatively felt his injured foot, and although it still hurt, he didn't think he had broken anything.

At midday, the boy and the dog returned together to the castle. When they arrived, they found the old man still lying where they had left him, his eyes open. His trousers were no longer wet and there was nothing protruding from his flies. The boy remained standing some distance away and the old man said:

'Sit down.'

'I don't want to.'

'I'm not going to hurt you.'

'You know they're looking for me. You're going to hand me over to them.'

'I have no intention of doing that.'

'Your intentions are exactly the same as theirs.'

'No, you're wrong.'

'Why have you brought me here, then?'

'Because it's a really remote spot.'

'Remote from what?'

'From other people.'

'Other people aren't the problem.'

'Anyone in these parts who sees you is likely to betray you.'

'Which is what you're going to do, right?'

'No.'

'You're just like all the others.'

'I saved your life.'

'So that you could get a reward, I suppose.'

The old man said nothing. Standing ten or so yards away, the boy kept restlessly pacing round and round in a tiny circle as if disappointment made him want to pee himself. The old man said:

'I don't know what you're running away from and I don't want to know.'

The boy stopped his pacing. The old man went on:

'All I know is that the bailiff doesn't have jurisdiction here.'

The boy heard the word 'bailiff' on the lips of the goatherd and felt the blood burning in his heels, felt the heat rising up from the ground and scorching him inside as only shame can. Hearing the name of Satan on the lips of another and feeling how that word tore down the walls he had built around his ignominy. Standing naked before the old man and the world. The boy retreated a few steps and crouched down. Leaning against the wall's warm, rough skin, he began to fit together, one by one, the pieces of the puzzle that the plain was handing him. He thought that in such a place, outside the jurisdiction of the bailiff and far from any inhabited villages, they could do with him as they wished. Only the stones would witness the inevitable brutal assaults and the death that would be sure to follow. He stood up.

'I'm leaving.'

'As you wish.'

The boy untied the tin from around the dog's neck and showed it to the goatherd.

'I'll take this.'

'It's yours.'

He poured water from the flask into the tin

and drank. Then he put the tin in his knapsack, squatted down and stroked the dog under the chin. Before leaving, he tightened the piece of string that served as his belt and glanced around him. The sky was a clear, blue vault. He smoothed his hair with his hands and, without turning to look at the goatherd, began heading north, leaving the castle behind him. The old man sat up to watch him leave. The dog gaily followed the boy, as if they were simply setting off together again to explore the fortress and its surrounds. It kept running from one side of the boy to the other, then stationed itself before him and put its paws on his thighs asking to be petted. The boy pushed the dog away, and the dog then stopped pestering him and trotted meekly after him. When they had gone some fifteen or twenty yards, the goatherd whistled, and the dog, its legs tense, paused and pricked up its ears. Then the boy bent down, put his hands about the dog's neck and whispered something into the dog's ear that made the dog relinquish its herding instincts and happily return to the castle wall.

The boy stood up, brushed off his trousers and felt a breath of warm air on the back of his neck. He sighed at the uncertainty of what lay ahead, and it was then that he heard the sound of an engine brought to him by that same breath of air. He turned and, in the distance, spotted a cloud of dust on the towpath. The heat haze was such that he couldn't actually see the surface of the earth or make out the precise origin of the noise that was growing ever clearer. He instinctively glanced back at the goatherd and saw that he too was kneeling, one hand shading his eyes, straining in the direction of that cloud of dust. The same wind that was bringing those men closer was also turning the thin pages of the Bible that now lay open on the ground. The goatherd signalled to him to get down out of sight.

The boy looked nervously about him in search of some escape route, but there was none. Behind him were the goatherd, the castle wall and its rubble. In every other direction lay the endless, pitiless plain where he would find no shelter. He crept back along the way he had come. He passed the old man and continued on until he was pressed against the wall.

'Hide.'

The boy lay flat on the ground and began to crawl along using his elbows. The pebbles dug into the skin of his arms and tore the sleeves of his shirt. He dragged himself along the whole wall round to the other side of the tower. Safe from the eyes of those men, he continued dragging himself through the rubble to the middle of the wall. The dog followed him, curious, waiting for the boy to throw it a stick or tickle it under the chin. It could so easily reveal his hiding-place. Squatting, with his back against the wall, he called to the dog and stroked it under the chin to pacify it.

When the search party left the towpath and headed up the track to the castle, the old man recognised the bailiff's motorbike. He was accompanied by two men on horseback, their horses' hooves striking sparks from the stones on the path.

The goatherd whistled and the dog stopped wagging its tail and pricked up its ears. It removed its head from the boy's hands and shot off round the wall to rejoin the old man, who was fumbling for something in the food pouch. As the men approached, the motorcycle engine backfired repeatedly, startling the pigeons nesting inside the tower.

The goats made way for the new arrivals. The old man dropped the last piece of dried meat at his feet. The dog sat down beside him and began licking and chewing that piece of sinewy flesh, which it would not take long to soften and swallow down.

The goatherd stood up to receive the men. He took off his hat and nodded a welcome.

One of the horsemen returned his greeting, touching his cap. The other man, who had a reddish beard, was already looking about him. Of the three, he was the only one to carry a weapon. A double-barrelled shotgun with a fancy inlaid butt. The bailiff turned off his engine and, even though the goats were still bleating and their bells tinkling, the old man felt as if a sudden absolute silence had fallen. The man took off his leather gloves and placed them, one beside the other, on the edge of the sidecar, fingers pointing inwards. Then, without getting off his bike, he removed first his goggles and then his helmet. His hair was drenched in sweat. He ran his hands over his face as if he were washing it and used his fingers to comb back his wet hair. From the sidecar he took out a brown felt hat, fanned himself with it for a few seconds, then put it on his head, carefully adjusting it over his eyes.

'Good afternoon, old man.'

'Good afternoon, sir.'

'Oh, so it's 'sir' now, is it?'

The bailiff's voice rang out among the stones. Hidden behind the wall, the boy felt the hairs on the back of his neck prickle and noticed a liquid warmth running down his tense legs, soaking his boots. The urine flowed over the leather and left a small damp patch on the ground. If he stayed where he was, they would be sure to find him the moment they came round to his side of the wall.

'It's a hot day.'

'Certainly is.'

The goatherd bent down, reached for the wicker handle of the flask, but lacked the strength to pick it up.

'Something to drink?'

'Don't mind if I do.'

The bailiff gestured to one of the men, who rode over to the goatherd. He was so big he made his horse seem small. He and the horse stood motionless next to the goatherd, who again bent down and tried to pick up the flask. The horse's belly was almost immediately above him. He took the flask in both hands and, closing his eyes, managed to lift it up to waist height. The rider reached down to receive the flask and rode back over to his boss, who uncorked it and took a long drink. The water ran down his chin and onto the dusty scarf round his neck. When he'd finished, he wiped his mouth with the back of his hand and returned the flask to the man who had brought it to him. That man then backed his horse up slightly and offered the flask to the other rider, who, instead, poured water over his face, neck and shirt.

'Go on, Colorao, have a drink!'

The red-haired man waved him away.

'Maybe the old man's got some wine.'

'He probably has.'

'I once met a man who hadn't drunk water in twelve years.'

'Oh, piss off.'

The bailiff turned and shot them a look that was enough to silence the two men immediately.

'We're after a boy who's disappeared.'

The goatherd stared at the horizon and frowned, as if trying hard to remember. He weighed up the situation presented to him by that arrogant bailiff.

'I haven't seen a living soul in weeks.'

'You must get lonely.'

'The goats keep me company.'

The red-haired man stood up in his stirrups as if to air his crotch or to peer over the wall. He scanned the wall from end to end for any clues. He was like an engineer come from the big city to certify officially that the castle was indeed a ruin.

'I'm sure they must give you no end of amusement.'

The rider who had picked up the flask gave a loud guffaw, and the bailiff allowed himself a faint smile. The old man remained utterly impassive, as did the man they called

Colorao, whose mind was clearly on other things. A few seconds passed in silence. The old man was just about managing to remain on his feet. The bailiff stroked his chin while he considered his next question.

'You've come a very long way with your goats.'

'I'm a goatherd, I have to keep moving on in search of fresh pastures.'

The red-haired man pulled on his reins and his horse reared up. He then rode towards the far end of the wall around which the boy had escaped, while the bailiff stayed behind with the old man. The latter forced himself not to follow the other man with his eyes because, if he did, that would only confirm what the bailiff already seemed to know. The red-haired man rode slowly round the wall, but by the time he had crossed to the other side, the boy was no longer there. He dismounted and walked the entire length of the wall, failing to notice the stones the boy had stained with blood from his grazed knees. When he reached the middle of the wall, however, he poked with his boot at the damp patch the boy had left on the ground. Resting the butt of his shotgun on the ground, he squatted down, picked up a pinch of sand with his fingers and sniffed it.

On the other side of the wall, the bailiff was

saying that this was hardly the leafiest of spots and that the same dry grass grew near the village. No one, he added, was going to travel that far just to buy his miserable milk; he should have listened when he took him to see the places where he should be pasturing his goats. He reminded him of his words at the time: 'Keep close to the village, but stay outside.'

The red-haired man was now heading for the door of the tower. Before entering, he stopped and inspected the curved walls rising up into the clear sky. Some of the pigeons had returned. He looked inside. There were bird droppings everywhere. The dried carcasses of pigeons, broken eggshells and the remains of a rodent devoured by some bird of prey. The parchment-like smell of the excrement masked the faint whiff of urine. He leaned further into the tower. Only the first step of the spiral staircase was intact. Beyond that, the steps still loosely attached to the wall rose up like the thread of a screw. The opening that gave access to the upper balcony was blocked by a mixture of pigeon faeces, feathers and twigs. Without that one source of light, anything in the tower more than nine feet above the ground was plunged in indecipherable darkness.

'Come out of there, you little bastard.'

The man's voice rose up through the tower and pierced the boy's skull, making his brain tremble. The boy had managed to climb onto one of the corbels and he shuddered so hard that he very nearly lost his footing and fell.

'Come out, you brat!'

When the bailiff and his other colleague joined him, he emerged from the tower and said:

'There's nowhere else he could hide for five miles around. He's either dead or he's hiding up there.'

'Now don't get in a state, Colorao. If he is hiding up there, he'll come out eventually.'

'It's pitch black, you can't see a thing.'

The bailiff pursed his lips and smoothed his hair, which was nearly dry now. He stepped back a little and studied the outside wall of the tower. He went over to the entrance. He poked at the sandy soil with his boot and uncovered the remains of the fire over which the old man and the boy had roasted the rabbit on the previous night. Turning to his men and pensively tapping his mouth with one hand, he looked at the red-headed man, but said nothing. Then he made another broader gesture, sending his two deputies off in different directions, while he remained standing at the entrance to the tower. From his inside pocket he removed a leather tobacco pouch and took out a packet of brown rolling papers, which he used to roll himself an almost perfect cigarette. When the men came back, they found their boss sitting on a stone, surrounded by threads of whitish smoke and amusing himself by flicking a silver lighter on and off.

'Not a sign of him, sir.'

The bailiff then gestured with his thumb at the wall behind him, and the two men again did as they were told, leaving their boss deep in thought. They found the goatherd sitting on the panniers, pretending to read the Bible.

'Come on, old man, up you get.'

The goatherd struggled to his feet and stood to one side. The men picked up the panniers and emptied them out, scattering their contents on the ground. The frying pan struck a stone and rang out like a bell. The tin container for the oil spilled its last drops onto the dust, but the goatherd did nothing. The men grabbed the panniers and the pack-saddle and dragged them over to the tower, where the red-headed man tore open the packsaddle and made a small pyramid out of the straw stuffing. On top he placed the rest of the saddle along with the panniers, forming a kind of pyre. The straw flared up as soon as the bailiff applied the lighter. The sheltering walls and the heat of the day did the rest. In a few seconds, the flames had leapt higher than the top of the entrance and were disappearing up into the tower. The men drew back so as not to be choked by the smoke and stood watching the flames devouring panniers and saddle, transforming them into thin black filaments. High up in the tower, a few pigeons could be heard cooing.

The boy didn't have time to feel afraid. His survival instincts took over, and initially he simply pressed his back against the wall as if that would somehow give him more space on the corbel on which he was perched. Enough space to be able to jump to the other side of the tower, above the smoke and the flames. The cells in his body were doing all his thinking for him and, among the various possibilities, they did not once consider that of dropping down onto the burning panniers and running out into the dry air of the plain. If it came to that, he would rather let the fire, like a blind, greedy ferret, bite him to death.

He was high enough up for the flames not to burn his feet, and the smoke had plenty of room to disperse above his head, enough to allow him a few more seconds before he suffocated and fell down onto the pyre below.

He felt along the wall behind him, although quite what he was hoping to find he didn't know. A door that did not exist or a mother who could lick his wounds. The flames were lighting up the inside of the tower now and when he saw a narrow vertical shape almost immediately opposite him, hope coursed through his body. It might be a window or the niche of a saint, like the ones he'd seen in his village on the stairs leading up to the shrine to Christ. He turned on his tiny perch and again felt along the wall, this time in search of handholds. There were cracks and indentations everywhere. Placing his hands inside one of those indentations or placing his feet in the gaps left in the wall where the staircase had crumbled away, he managed to advance up the remaining steps. He had, by now, lost all sense of time and had no idea how long it took him to reach that shadowy shape. It was an arrow slit blocked with stones. Perched on the triangular sill, he scrabbled desperately at the stones. The accumulated smoke had almost reached him. Two of the stones dropped down onto the fire below. Fortunately for him, the bailiff was sitting a little way away from the door, calmly smoking, and his men were further off still, chatting and expecting a body to fall, not a stone.

With the smoke already warming his back and hampering his every movement and intention, he managed to press his face to that opening in the wall and, at last, take a deep breath. The smoke also began to escape through that same opening and, for a few endless seconds, his mouth had to compete for air with those grey billows that were making his eyes sting and his skin smart. He pressed his face so hard against the stone that the blisters left by the sun on his cheekbones burst. At one point, he swallowed some smoke and, so as not to betray his presence to those waiting outside, he had to turn his head in order to cough inside the tower. Gradually, the smoke dissipated and he could move away from the arrow slit. He touched his skin with his black fingers and it stung.

Once the panniers were nothing but a heap of incandescent threads, the bailiff went back to the entrance to the tower and again gazed upwards. He finished his cigarette and stubbed it out on the ground, then told his men it was time to leave. However, the red-headed man joined him at the entrance to the tower and listened hard. He came out and whispered in the bailiff's ear that perhaps they should wait a little longer. His boss looked annoyed, but with a resigned wave of his hand, once more sat down on the stone and rolled himself another cigarette. The red-headed man went back to his companion and continued talking to him in a low voice, one of them keeping watch on the tower and the other on the plain towards the south. They were like relatives waiting impatiently for a funeral service to be over so that they could get back to the bar for a drink.

When the bailiff had finished his cigarette, he threw it down next to the first one and stubbed it out with his boot. He adjusted his hat and walked round the wall, without saying a word. The man watching the tower nudged his colleague and together they followed their boss. At that moment, their horses were grazing alongside the goats, and the old man was praying, his eyes shut.

6

The boy stayed in his hiding-place long after
the wild bleating of the goats, the men's
voices and the roar of the departing
motorbike had ceased. The toxic cloud of
smoke had finally gone, and the boy imagined
the pigeons' eggs ruined by the fire: their
blackened shells and, inside, the half-hatched
chicks. His legs ached after hours spent
crouched on the sill, but he decided to put up
with it for a while longer, wanting to be
absolutely sure that when he did come down
the bailiff would not be waiting for him
outside. Smoke-blackened but alive, he
allowed the hours to pass, unable to interpret
the meaning of the torture to which he had
been submitted. Had they set fire to the tower
because the goatherd had directed them there
or had they simply considered the tower to be
the only possible hiding-place?

Through the arrow slit, he watched the
evening coming on and was conscious of his
horribly taut skin and his gurgling stomach,
but now, after so long in one position, he
could no longer feel his bent legs or his
cramped muscles. There was no sound from

the goatherd. He fell asleep.

A noise woke him in the middle of the night. A muffled cry that rose up from the foot of the tower. The walls smelled of stale smoke, his skin still felt uncomfortably tight and his mouth dry. He squinted out through the arrow slit. In the pale light of the crescent moon, the plain was almost blue. The voice calling to him grew louder, but no clearer.

'Are you there, boy?'

It was the old man. The boy heard a cough and, shortly afterwards, the dull thud of a body falling to the ground. In the darkness of the tower, the stones felt greasy to the touch and he had to use the hard tips of his boots to feel for places stable enough to bear his weight. He took longer to descend than he would have liked and, when he finally reached ground level, he found the old man lying inside the base of the tower. He tried to wake him by tugging at his sleeve and moving his head from side to side, but received no response. He pressed his ear to the old man's chest to see if his heart was still beating, but could hear nothing. When he touched the old man's chest, it felt wet and sticky. He decided to drag him out of the tower by the legs so that he could see what was wrong with him by the scarce light of the moon. After great effort, though, all he could manage was to drag him as far as the entrance to the tower. Once outside, he put his face close to the goatherd's mouth and was able to confirm that he was at least still breathing albeit very feebly and irregularly. He could still not establish the exact cause of his collapse.

He spent the night next to the old man's motionless body. A warm breeze was blowing, bringing with it the bleating of a few nervous goats. The man's forehead was burning hot and he kept moaning in his sleep, a dull, continuous drone.

The boy was so exhausted that he woke only when it was already late morning. That was when he realised what had happened. The old man was still lying motionless by his side, covered only by the tattered remains of his clothes. Before beating him, the bailiff and his men had removed his jacket, leaving only his shirt. Where they had beaten him hardest, the cloth was stuck to his skin. His face was smeared with dried blood. His poor lips were covered in sores and red gashes, his closed lids as swollen as ripe figs. His limbs were bruised and the red weals on his side resembled extra ribs. The boy again tried to wake him, but the man did not respond. He pulled hard on his arm in an attempt to get him to sit up, but it was as if the old man's body were nailed to the floor of the tower. He slapped his face, and only then did the old man give any sign of life.

'Don't hit me, boy. I've had quite enough of that.'

In the old man's prostrate condition, with his eyes closed and his voice blurred, it seemed as if it wasn't him who was speaking, but his mind. The boy shook his head in a gesture that, far from releasing the tension he felt, only increased it. Then he covered his face with his hands and ran his rough palms over his skin. Incapable of taking in what had happened, he felt an urge to burst into tears, to cry out or even to inflict harm on himself.

'Bring me some water.'

The boy ran off. On the other side of the wall, half a dozen goats, their throats slit, lay in the area that had been shrouded in shadow on the previous afternoon. Their fly-studded wounds were like broad chinstrap smiles. The flies, often mounted one on top of the other, swarmed insalubriously over the wounds, doubtless depositing both eggs and infections. The three surviving goats were grazing nearby, indifferent to the massacre of their fellows and focused entirely on the needs of their own stomachs. The donkey was standing some way off. There was no sign of the dog or the billy goat.

The contents of the panniers were

scattered near the wall: the empty olive oil can, the frying pan, various rags, the crook and the shearing scissors; the plundered basket of raisins and the tobacco pouch turned inside out. He found the flasks uncorked and fallen on the ground. He tried each in turn, but only a few drops of water came out.

He carried them over to where the old man was lying and placed them upside down before him. The old man gave a snort of despair or resignation and seemed to want to close his eyes more tightly, as if this news made his weals burn still more intensely. In the face of this bottomless pit of pain, the boy felt that had the old man not been in such a state of extreme debilitation, he would gladly have killed himself.

'Milk one of the goats.'

The boy decided not to use the method employed by the goatherd, imagining that it would take too long to fix the bucket firmly in the ground and tether the goat's back legs to the rods. He found the tin where he had thrown it down when he first spotted the bailiff and the two men. He wiped it clean on the tail of his shirt and went over to where the goats were grazing. He crept up to one of them, but, as soon as the creature noticed him, it ran away. He went over to the next one, but with the same result. He spent quite a while chasing after them, but they slipped from his fingers like mercury. He went back to the wall to fetch the goatherd's crook and tried to remember how the old man had used it. He put it under his arm as if he were Don Quixote with his lance and set off towards the goats. The crook, however, was heavier than he thought and, as he walked, one end tipped forward and became stuck in the earth. He picked it up again and, gripping it firmly with both hands, approached his prey from behind. He slipped the crook between the animal's legs, but the goat took fright and fled. After several attempts, he resorted to the rather clumsier method of running after them and using the crook to trip them up. When this method finally succeeded, he threw down the crook, leapt on the goat and pinned it to the ground.

Then, grabbing one of the goat's hind legs, he dragged the creature over to the wall. Forced to walk backwards, the goat stumbled and fell every few yards, but the boy persisted, pulling at the goat as if he were lugging a great sack full of rabbits. Having wasted a lot of time just trying to catch the goat, he now had to milk it. He would have liked to present himself at the tower bearing a tinful of milk within minutes of receiving his orders. Just to prove to the old man that he had made good use of his time with him, and that, without him realising, he had been observing his every move and had absorbed some of his knowledge. However unconsciously, he wanted the old man to feel proud of him. He tied the goat's hind legs together, then tethered it to a rock. Placing the tin under the goat's udder, he knelt down. The first kick landed square in his stomach and the second on one cheekbone. The wound that had reopened when he'd pressed his face to the arrow slit began bleeding profusely. He fell back, winded, unable to fill his lungs. All the breath knocked out of him. He got up and, mouth open, managed to gulp down the air he needed. After several deep breaths, he recovered sufficiently to approach the animal again and give it a kick in the ribs. The goat bleated, then immediately resumed its search for food. The boy touched his raw cheekbone and his fingers slithered over a bone he could no longer feel. He looked at his fingers and saw that they were stained bright red. Like those gleaming toffee apples you buy at fairs. He didn't really have time to think, but the throbbing in his face was a painful reminder of the hours he had spent in the tower. His skin smeared with soot, his cheekbone burning from being pressed hard against the stone arrow slit. His hair, which was now the texture of tow, stank of stale smoke, a stench that would take him a lifetime to get rid of.

On the other side of the wall, however, he heard the old man moan and immediately dismissed his own aches and pains. He searched about for some bits of straw and placed them before the goat, then he positioned the tin under its udder and again knelt down. He grabbed the teats with his bloodied hands and tugged. The teats stretched as if they were made of warm rubber, but no milk came out. He squeezed and massaged the teats. He spat on his palms and rubbed them together forming a film of blood, soot and saliva. He started again. His fingers moved roughly over the teats until a few drops fell onto the ground. The goat continued to munch on the straw. It took the boy quite a while to achieve anything resembling a flow of milk. The tin was too small and, at first, he couldn't direct the stream directly into it, the milk dribbling onto the dust. He then held the mug immediately under the teat and milked using just one hand. When he had a couple of inches of liquid in the tin, he stood up and went back to the old man.

By the time he had caught and milked the goat, the sun had risen above the wall and begun to beat down on the tower. He found the goatherd lying, unprotected, in the sun. He appeared to be unconscious, and the boy feared that he had arrived too late. He jiggled the old man's arm and again slapped his face, but this time got no reaction. He decided to drag him into the shade. He grabbed him under the arms and pulled, but the old man was too heavy. He paused for breath, filled by a feeling of utter exhaustion and by a desperate thirst that had been building for many hours, but which circumstances had prevented him from quenching. He drank down all the milk in the tin and, even when there was not a drop left, remained standing with the tin pressed against his face.

He set off across the dry clods of earth in search of the donkey, who was attempting to graze on what was now only a distant memory of ancient furrows. Evidence that someone had been there before them, trying to claw something out of the soil that the plain was still jealously keeping to itself. The ruined castle bore witness to that. He returned, pulling the donkey by the frayed rope that hung down from the halter. It was a resigned, docile animal, with ulcers on its pasterns where it had been hobbled. It had a few bald patches here and there and some remnants of dried mud on its hooves. The marks left by the pool that had once existed around the reed bed.

The rope was far too short to tie around the old man's body; the boy needed something longer. He didn't find what he needed, but next to the old man's head, he found instead the bailiff's two brown cigarette ends. He imagined the three men blithely smoking as they watched the panniers burn, and instinctively he gritted his teeth.

He tied the rope around the old man's ankles, but the rope was so short that, when he had managed to tie a knot, the old man's boots were almost level with the donkey's mouth. The boy pushed against the donkey's chest, forcing it reluctantly backwards. The donkey brayed right in his ear, and the noise drilled into his brain. They managed to move a couple of yards. The goatherd's lifeless arms were drawn backwards in the process. Like the rough surface of a threshing board, the grit and pebbles from the crumbling wall stuck into the old man's flesh. He groaned out loud, and the boy put his ear to the goatherd's mouth and heard his irregular, but nonetheless encouraging, breathing.

He ran to the other side of the wall and returned with the saddlecloth. He tried and failed to place this between the old man's back and the ground, and opted instead to clear away all the debris that lay between them and the shade. The sun making his scalp sting. The old man's skin red and swollen. Flies like black teeth. He needed to stop and rest, but the old man's need was greater. He crawled along on all fours, clearing a path through the dust, casting aside any pebbles or bits of mortar. Then he again pushed against the donkey's chest and, at the first movement, the old man writhed helplessly, his groans now inaudible, his feet raised up by the rope, his back scraping over the ground and his arms flailing back and forth like unmanned rudders. A procession of the dead.

He placed the blanket on the ground in front of the blocked-off door to the castle, and dragged the old man over there. Pulling alternately on the man's arms and legs, he managed to make him as comfortable as possible. He raised the old man's head by placing a flat stone under the blanket and then prepared himself to hear whatever the goatherd had to tell him.

★   ★   ★

He granted the goatherd's first wish with heartening speed and efficiency, swiftly returning with half a tin of milk. He prised

119

open the old man's mouth with his fingers and administered tiny amounts of milk. The goatherd's Adam's apple moved up and down beneath the worn skin of his throat, and the hairs of his beard moved too like a bed of seagrass at the mercy of the currents. Then, when the old man gestured to him to stop, he raised the tin to his own lips and drank what was left in one gulp.

With his back to the old man, he tried to pee into the tin, but with scant success. For days now, he had hardly peed at all. Nevertheless, he managed to produce a little dense, yellow liquid that stank of ammonia. He turned to the old man again and, using a tattered piece of cloth torn from his trousers and dipped in the urine, he cleaned the old man's wounds. He felt the old man flinch at every touch and saw tears leak out from beneath his closed eyelids. At one point, the old man grabbed the boy's arm, begging him to stop. The boy waited for as long as the old man maintained his grip, then, when his grip slackened, he resumed his work, which had been the goatherd's second request. When he finished, he tried to get up, but the old man's hand still held fast to his elbow. So he placed the tin on the ground, lay down beside the goatherd, and they both fell asleep.

7

When he opened his eyes, the brief shadow cast by the wall had grown wider and longer, stretching out before them towards the empty horizon. The old man was lying awake by his side, hands folded on his chest and eyes fixed on the sky as if he wanted his gaze to linger for ever among the machicolations and corbels above. The boy sat up and gazed off into the distance. The old man spoke:

'How many goats are there left?'

'Three.'

'The billy goat doesn't count.'

'He's not here.'

The old man closed his eyes and sighed.

'Did they kill him too?'

'I don't know. I've only seen dead nanny goats so far.'

'Take another look.'

The boy got to his feet and surveyed the area before them. He counted the bodies one by one, pointing with his finger.

'Yes, six dead and all of them nanny goats. The dog and the billy goat have both disappeared.'

The old man thought that, sooner or later,

121

the dog would return from wherever it had gone. As for the billy goat, he assumed the men had taken it for its horns. Perhaps the bailiff would sacrifice the goat and add its head to his other trophies.

'You must go and find water as soon as possible.'

'If you're thirsty, I can milk one of the goats. I know how to do it now.'

'They're the ones who need the water.'

The boy took the milking pail and set off to fetch the water. A few yards from the well, he saw several crows perched on the edge. When he got there, he shooed the birds away with his hand and peered in. He heard the sound of buzzing and feared the worst. The scarce light entering the well was just enough for the boy to make out the decapitated corpse of the billy goat floating in the water, its stomach ripped open. All the flies in the area had gathered for the feast. They came and went like guests at a party. The arch over the well was thick with black dots.

It was almost dark by the time he got back. He told the old man what he'd found, and the old man gave a deep sigh at the thought of what awaited them. For the first time, the boy saw despair on the goatherd's face.

'Don't worry,' said the boy, 'we're bound to find some water nearby.'

'No, there isn't any.'

'How do you know?'

'I know.'

'We'll go somewhere else then.'

'I can't go anywhere.'

The boy fell silent. If the goatherd couldn't move, then he would have to go in search of water on his own. He remembered the previous days, the sunstroke, the thirst, the night-time walks, and felt afraid. He had only survived then because the goatherd had been there.

'You'll have to go for water on your own.'

'I don't know where to go.'

'I'll tell you.'

'I'm afraid.'

'Nonsense, you're a brave lad.'

'No, I'm not.'

'You've come this far.'

'Only because you were there.'

'No, because you had determination.'

The boy didn't know what to say.

'Have you seen the halo surrounding the head of the Christ up above?'

'Yes, it has three rays of light coming out of it.'

'That's right, well, one represents memory, another understanding and the third determination.'

The boy looked up. He could see the figure

silhouetted black against the evening light and could make out the tunic, the hands and the rays. The boy was touched by what the old man had told him and, for a moment, forgot his worries.

'Christ suffered too.'

'But I don't want to suffer any more.'

'Then we'll just have to stay here and die of thirst. That'll soon put an end to your suffering.'

★   ★   ★

The old man told him that, to the north, there was a village with a well. He wasn't sure exactly how far away it was, but it would take the boy a few hours to get there. He would have to set off soon, along with the donkey, but before the boy left, he still had work for him to do at the castle.

The first task was to bring him the corpse of the brown nanny goat. Then he ordered him to take the collars and bells off the other dead goats and drag their bodies as far as possible from the castle.

It took him until dark to drag the bodies over the stony ground. Every now and then, he would pause and touch his cheekbone with the back of his hand, then wipe away the sweat from his brow. After more than a day in the sun, the intestines of the dead goats were beginning to swell, lethal gases accumulating in the stewpots of their entrails. The crowds of vultures and crows that would soon arrive would be visible for many miles around. Black feathers circling endlessly above the dusty earth. For a moment, the boy considered burning the bodies and thus avoiding any possibility of attracting scavengers and disease, but realised at once that, in the middle of the night, the glow would be seen from far and wide. With luck, the bailiff would assume he had not survived his trial by fire in the tower. However, given the state in which they had left the goatherd, a pyre of burning goats would inevitably lead them to believe that he, the boy, was still alive.

When he had finished piling up the corpses, he went back to the castle and sat down by the old man. For a while, neither of them spoke, the old man too absorbed in his pain, the boy exhausted by his efforts. He was just about to fall asleep, when he felt the goatherd's hand on his elbow.

Following the goatherd's precise instructions, he sharpened the old steel knife, a tool with a blunt point, a notch at one end, and a hilt wound round with string. He used a stone to grind the blade until it had a silvery edge to it. Then he placed the brown goat on its back and, gripping its head between his knees, plunged the knife through its slit throat and sliced down its chest as far as its udder. He had watched his mother gutting rabbits and hares. He himself had killed quail by breaking their necks, but this was entirely different; this was a much larger animal from whose belly oozed bluish innards that slithered out of his hands. He plunged in the knife again to open the goat's swollen abdomen. However primitive the blade, it cut through the stomach lining like a knife through butter. The stench that burst forth rushed through him like a damned soul in flight, making a deep impression in the fresh clay of his memory. He looked away and met the gaze of the goatherd, who was watching in silence from where he lay. He felt the goatherd's eyes urging him on. The boy's clumsy hands were his hands.

That first blast of putrefaction soon dissipated. Before him lay a kind of tub overflowing with iridescent blues and creamy whites, with globular shapes that twisted and turned in every possible direction. The old man was expecting him to gut the goat, then cut it up just as he himself had done with the rabbit and the rat. So overwhelmed was the boy by the complexity of the goat's entrails that he didn't know what to do. Sleeves rolled up, knife in one hand, he looked at the goatherd and shrugged.

'Stick your hand underneath its guts, feel for the point where they begin and make a cut right there.'

* * *

An hour later, the guts were lying next to the pile of corpses like some goatishly ironic joke or a Dantesque vision of the future or a warning from a hit man. On the way, he had to stop several times to pick up bits of intestine that slipped from his embrace.

During the hours that followed, the old man continued issuing orders to the boy, who silently carried them out like a tool being wielded by the mind of another.

He began carving up the goat, dislocating its legs and then crudely deboning them. He cut as many slices as he could from the resulting lump of meat, placed them on a stone and salted them liberally. At one point, he made the mistake of wiping the sweat from his brow. The salt penetrated the wounds on his sweat-moist cheeks. The pain was such that he clenched his eyes tight shut and felt a kind of hollow forming inside him. He didn't cry out. He merely gazed up at the sky and wept like a St Sebastian full of arrows, his hands burning and his skin cauterised by the salt. He spun round and round, holding his hands out, palms facing him, as if shading the glowing lamp of his face. Had there been a swamp nearby, he would gladly have hurled himself into it. The old man watched this agonising dance and even tried to get up, not that he could have done much to help. The boy knelt down and fell back on the ground, still keeping his hands away from his face. The old man reached out one arm to him and held it there for as long as he could. Then he slowly let it fall and closed his eyes.

In the silky light of the half-moon, the boy unwound the string from the handle of the knife, his eyes still red and his face still stinging. Having hunted around for a couple of sticks and stuck each in a hole in the wall, he then strung a piece of string between the two sticks and on it hung the strips of meat. The result drew a grotesque smile on the bluish stones, a smile that soon attracted the flies. Then he picked up his tools and arranged them around the old man, as if he were a sailor shipwrecked on a beach. Again following the goatherd's instructions, he rounded up the three surviving goats and tied them together using the collars from the bells of those who had been killed. Then he tethered one end to a nearby rock so that they were all within reach of the goatherd's crook. He put the saddle pad and the blanket on the donkey, tied the two empty flasks together and slung them over the donkey's back like a pair of boots.

By dawn, they had finished their preparations for the journey. There was scarcely any breeze, and the stones of the castle wall were quietly doing penance for the heat they had absorbed during the day. The old man and the boy ate what little remained to them: a few crumbs of bread, a handful of raisins salvaged from the ground and some wine. When they had finished, the old man asked the boy to sit down next to him.

'I'm going to teach you how to milk a goat properly.'

The boy looked at the goatherd in surprise. At any other moment, those words would have filled him with pride. However, it seemed strange to him that, in their current situation, the goatherd should want to waste precious time on such a thing.

'It's getting late. If I don't leave soon, it will be daylight.'

'I know it's late.'

'You can teach me when I get back.'

Several black birds flew past, heading for the well. Their wings creaked as they flew across the dark sky. The donkey, head down, was moving forlornly about in front of them. The boy's eyes filled with tears, but he didn't cry or even sniffle. He simply stayed where he was next to the bent old man, feeling the sky brushing the earth and aware of an ancient murmur emanating from the rocks. He imagined a watermill in a beech wood and horizons like the jagged blade of a saw. The sky penetrating and piercing the earth, and the mountains rising up to meet it. The home of the gods. The paradise the priest had so often spoken of. A green carpet on which the trees rested nonchalantly, unaware of their own lush foliage. Maples, fir trees, cedars, oaks, pines, ferns. Water springing eternally up between the rocks. Cool moss covering everything. Pools where transparency was the norm and whose stony beds glinted in the sun. Rushing streams temporarily tamed and on which the light traced rainbow spirals.

The boy hastily swallowed his tears and got up. Without even bothering to untie it from the others, he led one of the goats over to the old man. Then he sat down next to him and waited while the old man placed the tin in its proper place. When he had done this, he asked the boy to take hold of the teats. The boy formed his hands into loose fists, put them around the teats and squeezed. Then the goatherd positioned the boy's thumbs so that the nails pressed the teats against his other fingers. He put his hands over the boy's hands and, without a word, manipulated the teats, making the milk flow freely. And in doing so, the old man passed on to the boy the rudiments of his trade, handing him the key to a knowledge that was at once vital and eternal. The key to extracting milk from animals or making a whole wheatfield grow from an ear of wheat. They had soon filled the tin and the empty oil bottle, leaving the goats completely dry. They kept the bottle for the old man's breakfast the next day and shared the milk in the tin between them.

Later, once he was mounted on the donkey, he took one last look at the goatherd, who was lying down now, his beard sticky with rivulets of dried milk. He appeared to be asleep or unconscious. A fine breeze touched the boy's cheek, reminding him that, only a while before, his face had been like a fiery planet.

'Be very wary of the people in the village.'

The old man's voice emerged from some indefinable place, from somewhere beyond exhaustion.

The boy turned his gaze north, towards his uncertain fate. Then he slung his knapsack on the packsaddle and dug his heels into the donkey's sides, to which the donkey responded

by emitting a series of sour belches and breaking into a trot that carried them away from
the castle.

8

The waxing crescent moon hung in a clear night sky. Thousands and millions of stars, many of them already dead, winked down at him from above. He had to head north along the towpath until he reached a lock. From there, he was to follow a gentle downhill path for about two hours until he came to a small oak wood, from where he would be able to see the village. The well was in the village. Assuming he didn't get lost, he should, according to the old man, be within sight of the houses by dawn.

Boy and donkey travelled beside the dried-up aqueduct, from which side channels occasionally branched off, only to vanish into the barren fields. Empty, bluish fields. From time to time, the boy nodded off and almost lost his balance. Then he would briefly become more alert and beat the donkey with his stick, and while this succeeded in eliciting protests from the poor, startled creature, it failed to make it trot any faster. The boy was aware that they were only moving at a walking pace, but he still preferred to ride rather than walk, so as to preserve the little strength he had for when they reached the well.

★   ★   ★

'Be very wary of the people in the village.' Each time the donkey stumbled, the boy would wake, pondering the old man's words with a mixture of disquiet and satisfaction. He didn't know if the goatherd had said this because his own life depended on him returning with the water or simply out of a desire to protect him. Then his neck would droop and his head would once again fall onto his chest and he would again become lost in the magma of his thoughts and memories. The hole he had dug, the palm tree, the poultice, the arrow slit, the goatherd's penis, the bailiff's cigarette ends.

The boy spotted the sluice during one of his brief waking moments and, after that, he did not fall asleep again. To urge the donkey on, he dug his heels into the donkey's sides and squeezed its flanks with his thighs, but received no response. When they arrived, he dismounted and, for the last few yards, led the donkey by its halter, before releasing it to nose around for dry stalks to graze on. The boy scrambled up the bank to the tank into which the water from the aqueduct had once flowed. The aqueduct formed a T-junction here. Two iron sluices operated by winding gear controlled the flow of water. From his vantage point, he looked southwards down the gap-toothed channel until it became lost in the darkness. The bottom of the aqueduct was nothing but dry mud. He turned then and looked north, where the path curved down towards the plain. No oak woods and no villages, only bare, eroded slopes ribbed with stones.

Just as the old man had predicted, the boy reached the wood shortly before sunrise. He tethered the donkey to the low branch of an oak tree and walked over the bed of serrated leaves and empty acorn cups as far as the northernmost edge of the wood. From that dark fringe of trees, he had a clear view of the village, which consisted of perhaps twenty houses, a single street and a church situated midway between the wood and the village. A few yards from the church was a cemetery, and above the cemetery wall he could see the swaying tops of three cypresses like upended paintbrushes. The same slight breeze stirred the branches above his head. The occasional empty acorn fell onto the soft ground that crunched underfoot, and he was reminded of his own empty belly. The village showed no signs of life. He could make out a few enclosures that might be corrals, but there were no sounds of any farm animals. Maybe it was deserted, he thought, or maybe it was simply too early for people to be up and about. He decided it would be best to make his first foray without the donkey. Then, if the conditions were right, he would return for the donkey, load it up with water and lead it back to the castle.

He emerged from the wood at the first light of day, taking care not to stumble. His boots still afforded his feet some protection from the ground, but the front part of one of the soles had come loose, allowing the boot to fill up with grit. When he crouched down to empty it out, he noticed that the backs of his hands were still smeared with soot and blood. He touched his cheekbones and felt the scabs that were beginning to form. He still stank to high heaven. The breeze veered slightly, and he could feel the cool dawn air through the tears in his trouser legs. If there were any dogs in the village, they would soon begin to bark.

The thought of dogs made his stomach contract, because the bailiff used to keep a black one as a guard dog. A Dobermann he called it. Pointed ears on a head that seemed carved out of stone, and a tar-black snout that would nose around among his clothes and make him tremble. The bailiff had often deliberately submitted him to the dog's presence whenever he resisted his desires. That thought was like a cold chisel cutting into his tender fontanelle or a sharp instrument gouging into his elbows in search of white bone. He hunched down until he was hugging his knees and, for the second time in a week, he peed his pants. The light was growing brighter around him, picking out new shapes in the landscape.

He covered the distance separating him from the cemetery on all fours. Sand clung to his damp crotch. When he reached the nearest wall, he stood up and circled round until he reached the westernmost corner. From there he could see some of the houses, but not the well, because the church was in the way. Head down, he crossed the area separating cemetery and church and got as far as the portico. As in his own village church, the pillars supporting the roof were connected by a continuous row of stone benches, interrupted at one point to provide access to the church. The area was carpeted with the leaves the wind had blown in from a nearby acacia tree and deposited in untidy piles around the benches. The door, hanging by one hinge, seemed about ready to fall off. He followed the filthy crumbling wall round to the apse. Broken tiles and bits of plaster littered the ground, and it was clear that the church was no longer in use. This was a discovery that both reassured and worried him in equal measure, because if no one was taking care of the church, that was because no one attended it any more, and he would probably not have to hide from anyone. On the other hand, the lack of inhabitants could also mean a lack of water. He positioned himself by the apse wall and from there, at last, had a panoramic view of the village. He saw sunken roofs and a few gaping windows, as well as a large wood-and-metal harvester like a Trojan horse devoured by scrub.

He entered the village by the same path that had led him into the oak wood, although, for the last stretch, he had chosen to go across the fields instead. On either side of the dirt road, he found either locked and barred houses or broken-down doors through which the same scene could be seen over and over: fallen beams that opened up great holes in the roof and shed light onto the piles of rubble beneath. Ceramic tiles with grubby, faded designs. The occasional photo of the king and queen or out-of-date calendars bearing advertisements for nitrates. Lumps of ceiling plaster mixed with wattle, and struts wound about with twine. From some façades drainpipes hung, their fixings having come loose from the walls, leaving indentations like bullet holes. Cavities left by crumbling plaster laid bare the skeletons of the houses, their thick wooden beams. He had a look at one such house. It smelled of darkness and rotten olives. Somewhere up in the roof he heard the fluttering of pigeons and their monotonous cooing.

Towards the far end of the village, the street opened out to form an irregular square, like the stopping-place for a caravan of pioneers. On one side was the well, from whose wrought-iron arch hung a pulley bereft of rope and bucket. He leaned over the granite rim, expecting the worst, but could make out nothing until his eyes grew accustomed to the darkness below. Only then could he see the brick wall and, about fifteen feet down, a kind of brick buttress that traversed the well from side to side. Below that, nothing. He dropped in a stone that bounced off the arch before continuing its descent. Immediately afterwards, he heard the dull splash of the stone hitting water. He threw in a few more stones to make sure. With his hands resting on the rim, he gave a sigh of relief, although he was all too familiar with abandoned wells and their bad water.

He visited various ruined houses, unwinding twine from the beams. Some was simply wound around, while some had been nailed to the wood with tin tacks. To remove the tacks he used one leaf from an old laminated spring he found lying around, until, finally, he had enough twine for his purposes. In the pantry, he found several suspiciously swollen cans. He placed one on the floor and, holding it with one hand, struck the lid with the sharp corner of a tile. Brown liquid spurted forth. The smell was so overpowering that he had to run out into the street to catch his breath. While he waited, he improvised a bucket by tying a twine handle to an earthenware pitcher. Then, using the same metal leaf, he opened the can fully, emptied out the contents and went back to the well.

The water he brought up was full of small white worms that moved by expanding and contracting like tiny springs. He poured a little water into the can to rinse it out, and when it was more or less clean, took off his shirt and placed it over the top of the can to act as a kind of filter. The worms writhed and leapt about on the cloth like tuna fish in a net. The first sip he took tasted slimy, but he was so thirsty that he threw caution to the wind and drank until he could drink no more.

He washed his smoke-stiffened face and, even though several hours had passed since the fire in the tower, the water still dripped black into the dust. He hauled up another pitcher of water and took off his trousers. While the water didn't wash away all the grime, it did refresh him and, for the first time since he had run away, he felt something akin to the comfort he had known at home with his family. The mixture of soot, dust, blood and urine ran in grubby streams down his legs. He emptied several pitchers of water over his head and, before going back to fetch the donkey, sat down on the rim of the well to rest.

He felt the first pangs when he was halfway between the village and the wood. The cramps in his stomach forced him to squat down on the path. He clutched his belly as he was gripped by continuous waves of contractions, a feeling like being kicked repeatedly in the gut. He lowered his trousers and defecated right there and then. He felt a momentary relief, and his stomach seemed briefly to return to normal. He wiped his bottom on a stone, but, as he was about to pull up his trousers, his legs gave way beneath him as a new wave of cramps took hold. He only just had time to pull down his trousers again before another stream of excrement covered the bottoms of his trousers and his heels. He felt an endless need to open his bowels as if inside his body, a tap had been turned on that he could not turn off.

He found the donkey grazing placidly, seemingly as happy to nibble on last spring's aborted oak leaves as it was to munch on tiny, crunchy wild asparagus shoots. The boy untethered it, climbed onto its back and headed off towards the path. They proceeded at the gentle pace dictated by the old donkey, whose swaying gait again sent tremors through the boy's stomach. Fortunately, he had nothing more inside him. After days spent out in the open, a whole night spent perched on the sill of an arrow slit, followed by another sleepless night on the trail of that half-putrid water, and now, having found the well and having been spared any dealings with the villagers, he felt so relaxed that, by the time they entered the village, he was asleep with his arms around the donkey's neck and with the hard frame of the saddle pad sticking into his stomach. As if endowed with the skills of a water diviner, the donkey headed straight along the street to the square, where the fallen pitcher had left a pool of water. When they arrived, the donkey stopped and reached down to lick the damp mud, almost propelling the boy forward over its head. However, the boy woke just in time to regain his balance. He then sat very erect on the donkey's back and stretched his arms up to the sky, fists clenched, then he unclenched them and felt something click in his solar plexus. He dismounted, and the first thing he did was to lower the pitcher down the well and give the donkey some water to drink. As soon as he placed the pitcher on the ground, the donkey thrust its muzzle into the pitcher's round mouth and lapped up all the water its tongue could reach. While the donkey was drinking, the boy considered removing the flasks, filling them up and then putting them back. He had seen similar wicker-covered flasks at home, usually filled with wine, and he reckoned they must hold at least five gallons of water each. In the end, though, he rejected this option as impracticable and decided instead to fill the flasks gradually, without taking them off the donkey's back. He accordingly spent the next hour drawing up water from the well and pouring a little into each of the flasks in turn, so that the load wouldn't become unbalanced. When he thought the flasks were half full, he decided to sit down and rest. He walked round the well, in search of shade, but the sun was so high there was scarcely any shade to be had. He could have gone into one of the houses, but, given the precarious state of most of the roofs, he dismissed this idea too. Instead, as he had on the long walk to the reed bed, he decided to use the donkey to protect him from the sun. He sat down, leaning his back against the stone wall of the well, holding the halter so that the donkey would not move away, and then promptly fell asleep.

He woke, feeling hot and agitated and with a feeling of dampness around his feet. He opened his eyes and found that his feet were buried in a heap of dung and urine deposited by the donkey, which was now standing a couple of yards from him, flicking away flies with its tail. He didn't know how long he had been sitting in the sun, but into his mind came memories of the goatherd's poultice and the dog licking his teeth. He felt slightly dizzy and, for a moment, his vision grew blurred. He leaned against the wall of the well to steady himself, and was filled with a sudden loathing for that beast of which all he had asked was a little shade, only to be denied even that. He strode over to the donkey and punched it hard on the muzzle. The animal merely shook its head, unmoved, whereas he felt a pain, like a cramp, shoot from his knuckles right up to his skull. He stood among those few ruined houses and gave an agonised cry which he kept up even when the pain in his bones had abated. A long howl that made him fall to his knees, exhausted, in the middle of the dusty square.

'You don't seem very happy.'

The boy started to his feet and backed away from that male voice, which had emerged from somewhere behind him. He hid behind the well and stayed there utterly still, playing for time while he listened, ears cocked, for any sounds of movement. For a few seconds all he could hear was the cooing of the pigeons in the roofs of the houses. Then came a creak as if from an axle, which he identified as coming from some sort of wagon. He assumed the man was a peasant farmer.

'Come out, boy. I'm not going to harm you.'

'I haven't done anything.'

'I know. I've been watching you since I saw you up at the church.'

The boy whirled around, as if expecting to see watchful eyes at every window.

'Please, just let me leave.'

'Come out, will you? Like I said, I'm not going to harm you.'

'No, I won't come out.'

The boy glanced towards the entrance to the village and considered escaping down the street, but the street was too long, and if the man had a shotgun, he would prove a very easy target. And even if he didn't get shot, walking to the castle in the heat of the day would be impossible. And if he returned with no water, the old man would die and so would he.

'How do I know you're not going to harm me?'

'You just have to look at me.'

★ ★ ★

The man had long, matted hair and a black beard, and wore only a tattered hessian tunic tied at the waist. His hands were not fully formed, and his legs had been amputated just below the knees. Frayed leather straps bound his thighs to a wooden plank fitted with four greasy ball bearings that served as wheels. The tension in the boy's muscles dissolved at once when he saw that the threat he had imagined was no threat at all, and then, as if he were studying a painting, he stood, hypnotised, staring at that peculiar body, from plank to head. He observed him as if through a tunnel of caulked walls, at the end of which the man and his plank seemed to form one being. Both plank and man were equally filthy, and not even the stink of urine and creosote he gave off could distract the boy, his senses numbed both by the sight of that strange creature and by his own now dry

146

effluvia of urine and sweat that had gradually been so absorbed into his pores that they seemed to form part of him.

'Do you like my chariot?'

The boy emerged reluctantly from his stunned state. After the initial shock, the blood was once more flowing aimlessly through his slack veins. The person talking to him proved so utterly inoffensive that the boy, confusing relief with rudeness, answered rather peevishly, forgetting that the man might easily be the owner of that well or have a pistol concealed beneath his tunic.

'I only took a little water.'

'That's all right. You can take as much as you want. Except, of course, the water's bad. It's probably already given you the shits.'

The boy said nothing, but instinctively clenched his buttocks.

'What are you doing here all alone?'

'I'm not alone. My father and brother are waiting for me in the oak wood up there.'

'And they sent you to fetch water, right?'

'Yes.'

'Well, go and get them. You can all eat at my inn. I won't charge you much.'

The boy looked around for some sign, some advertisement, but saw only houses that were either locked up or derelict. He pulled a sceptical face.

'It's over there,' said the man.

The cripple craned his neck to one side, indicating the road leading north out of the village. The boy thought he must be lying, because no one in his right mind would keep an inn in a place like that.

'It's true. You may not believe it, but this road leads straight to the capital. Once the drought ends, the traders and the travellers will soon return.'

The boy looked in the direction indicated by the cripple. At the end of the street there was one not entirely dilapidated house, with its front door standing open. If that really was the inn, it must be very cheap indeed.

'We're in a hurry. We don't have time to stop and eat.'

'At least buy a loaf.'

'I don't have any money.'

'At least take a few biscuits. I want you to remember me the next time you're passing.'

The boy didn't want to go with him. He was afraid there might be someone else waiting in the house, but the cripple spoke so seductively of bread and biscuits. The boy's mouth watered at the thought. He remembered the *turrón* they used to eat at Christmas and felt tempted to follow the man, but stopped himself. How could that man make biscuits, he thought, when he had only four fingers? He decided that he would keep a close eye on him while he continued filling the flasks, then go back the way he had come.

'They're made with almonds and sugar,' the cripple added.

⋆   ⋆   ⋆

The boy followed him down the street. The man propelled himself along with a pair of wooden sticks, which he gripped firmly, despite his lack of fingers. Halfway there, he got stuck in a patch of soft sand and had to reverse and skirt round the obstacle.

'Sometimes I hitch up the pig and get him to pull me along. That's much better. Using these sticks really wears out your hands and arms. What I wouldn't give for a donkey like yours.'

The boy imagined the pig in full harness, like a trotting horse, with the cripple behind him strapped onto his plank. The last time the boy had seen a pig was four winters ago. His father had slaughtered it with the help of another man from the village. His mother had made sausages from it while he and his brother stirred the blood with their hands.

Outside the house was a rather stunted vine trellis beneath whose shade, according to the cripple, the muleteers used to sit. There was a window on either side of the door, with a stone bench beneath each window. A diamond-shaped pattern was pricked out on each leaf of the closed green metal shutters. The house was dark inside and, as he stood at the front door, the boy could see nothing of the interior. The cripple went in and disappeared into the gloom. The boy tethered the donkey to a metal ring next to one of the windowsills. He picked up his knapsack and, before going into the house, glanced at the heavily laden donkey. It occurred to him that, even if he would only be stopping for a short time, he should at least relieve it of some of the weight. He tried to lift one of the flasks, but, although he could lift it, he imagined that, if he removed it, the other flask, to which it was attached, might unbalance the load. Then he glanced down at his boot, still wet from the donkey's urine, and then at his knuckles and remembered that sharp pain up his arm, which he could still feel, and the long time the donkey had left him exposed to the sun. No, you can wait, he thought.

The cripple appeared round the door.

'Are you coming in or not?'

The boy nodded. The man went back into the house, and the boy cautiously approached the front door. As he stood under the lintel, he felt the cool air emanating from the dark interior, bringing with it various meaty aromas. You went straight from the street into the main room, which was lit only by the tongue of light coming in through the front door. The room smelled of worm-eaten wood and dried intestines. The air was perfumed with olive oil and vinegar. Suddenly the cripple opened a shutter at the far end of the room and light flooded in, revealing the details of its hidden corners. Strings of sausages, shoulders of ham, smoked ribs, cured pork cheek. At the back, a couple of large sacks of flour and a barrel. Bowls of almonds and bottles of wine. A round wooden box full of salted sardines arranged like the spokes of a wheel and various slabs of salt cod hanging from a beam. Bags of dried chestnuts, black-eyed peas and sugar and, beyond that, behind a curtain, a door that promised still more food.

'I sell provisions to travellers too.'

★   ★   ★

The boy ate a slightly rancid cabbage-and-bean stew, wiping the enamel plate clean with large slices of bread. He asked for some water, but the cripple told him that the water in the barrel had not yet been boiled. Not wanting to wait for the boiled water to cool, he washed down his meal with half a tumbler of rough wine, which the cripple gladly offered him. Followed by some cakes, dates and honey-roasted almonds.

While the boy was devouring all this food, the man explained that the few remaining villagers had left when the well stopped providing them with drinkable water. He spoke, too, about the traders who passed through the village and about the inn. It had been run by his brother, and he, his sister-in-law and his two nephews had all lived there. When the drought came, they told him they were going to the city to find work and would come back to fetch him in a cart once they were settled. 'That was a year ago,' he told him. While the man was talking to him about muleteers, wool merchants and goat's cheese, the boy fell asleep at the table.

He dreams he's being pursued. The usual dream. He's running away from someone he never sees, but whose hot breath he can feel on his neck. Someone who speeds up when he does and stops when he stops. He runs down the rain-wet streets of an unfamiliar city. Not that he had ever left his village or even seen photographs of a big city. Drenched, empty streets where the light from the street-lamps bounces off the cobblestones, which gleam black as polished coal. He runs round corners and down alleyways that grow ever narrower and darker, the footsteps of his pursuer always at his back. He goes into a house and walks down corridors lit by flickering gas lamps that give off a yellowish glow. The warm, sticky air clings to his clothes, slowing him down. He can hear someone breathing behind him. He goes into a room where the only light that exists is outside the windows. He opens doors that give onto low-ceilinged rooms of ever-diminishing size. Finally, he's lying face down on a damp, insect-ridden wooden floor. The ceiling is so low that it touches his back. The air is like thick axle grease now. Immobile, trapped, he feels as if he were sinking ever deeper into the bowels of the earth, in search of molten magma. He is momentarily aware that he is lying in his coffin, then a sudden spasm makes his head thud onto the table.

*   *   *

When he woke, he was alone, with his left wrist manacled to an iron pillar. He had a slight gash on his forehead. His head and his stomach ached. He felt an urgent need to empty his bowels, but couldn't move more than a yard. The windows were closed again and the only available light came through the pinprick pattern on the shutters. He tried to slip his hand out of the manacle, but it was too tight. Stretching his arm as far as he could, he managed to reach out one leg and touch the window with the tip of one foot. This awkward position made him belch, and he felt all the acid from the food rising up into his throat, leaving a taste of bile in his mouth. He could tap the window very lightly with his boot, but not hard enough to break it. He groped around him for some helpful object, but there was only the wicker chair he was sitting on. He picked this up with his free hand and tried to use it to reach the window, but it was too heavy. Instead, he slipped one hand through the slats in the back of the chair and, gripping the seat with his hand, managed to raise it above his head. With eyes closed, he smashed it down on the table, breaking it into more manageable pieces. He kept on smashing until all he had in his hand were the two slats from the back of the chair and one leg to which these were attached. He used the leg to break the glass of the closed window and push open the leaves of the shutters. The light that entered was not the same as the bright morning light that had flooded in when the cripple had opened the shutters earlier, but it was enough to illuminate the room.

The first thing he realised was that the donkey was not where he had left it. He saw, too, that the manacle around his wrist consisted of an iron ring with a padlock on it. He tried to break open the padlock by striking it on the table, then on the floor, but without success. He looked around him in search of something that might help, but could see only food and drink. Having trudged across that vast plain on a meagre diet of almonds and goat's milk, there he was surrounded by food, but manacled to a pillar.

He tried to think through his situation: he was a prisoner, the cripple had disappeared, and the donkey wasn't where he had left it. Despite being possibly the only person in the province with enough food to last a whole year, the cripple had fled, leaving him a captive. He imagined the plank on its ball-bearing wheels being pulled along by the pig, just as the cripple had described to him. Or, the boy wondered, had the cripple's desire for freedom been so great that he had abandoned everything and made off with the old donkey? At least he hadn't killed him in order to do so. He thought of the goatherd. He imagined him lying at the foot of the castle wall, about to breathe his last. The crows perched on the head of the Christ figure or on one of the corbels, awaiting their moment. The goats maddened by the lack of water. He realised that if he didn't escape, he might well meet the same fate. He would die of hunger and thirst, chained to that pillar. Seeking consolation, he thought of his family, but his family were the reason he was there.

On the table was the plate from which he had eaten, surrounded by splinters of wood and bits of broken chair. With one hand he cleared a space so that he could sit down and only then did he notice something that his urgent desire to eat had prevented him from seeing before. On one corner of the table, next to an enamel bowl, was a tin ashtray. It contained a single brown cigarette end, the sight of which made the blood drain from his face and his stomach contract with fear. Then he understood why the cripple had fled, and the only thing he felt then was a need to get out of there and catch up with the man who was intent on betraying him.

He tried to put his ideas in order. He didn't know how long he had been asleep, nor how much time had passed since the cripple had left. All he knew was that he had to reach him before he found the bailiff. He again struggled with the manacle, trying various positions that would allow him to remove his hand, until the metal, cutting into his flesh, became too painful. He looked around for some useful implement, but the cripple had made sure to remove any object that could be turned into a tool. The only thing he could reach was the cured meat hanging on hooks from the wall, doubtless left there by his jailer in order to keep him alive until he returned with the bailiff. He wondered how much of a reward they were offering.

He moved as close as he could to the wall in order to reach the meat. He tugged hard at a piece of salt pork, tearing it off the hook on which it hung. He squeezed and massaged the meat with his hands, rubbed the fat onto his manacled wrist and tried to extricate his hand by sliding it out — to no avail. He then energetically greased the metal ring itself, as if that might soften it. The rancid smell of the grease mingled with the stench given off by his own body. He then grasped the metal ring with his free hand and pulled with his trapped hand, meanwhile turning it inside the ring. He tried gripping the ring between his knees and pulling with both hands, but this proved so painful he had to stop.

With his elbows resting on the table and the manacle slightly below his wrist, he then worked on flexing his thumb. He again greased and massaged the base of the joint, feeling for it much as his mother used to do when carving a chicken. Then, with his fingers squeezed together on either side of his thumb, and when both hand and brain were ready, he rolled up the napkin he had used earlier and placed it between his teeth. Finally, he hooked the ring over a metal fitting on the table and pulled as hard as he could. He felt the ring tearing the skin on his thumb and felt how his greased knuckles were pushed together to fit the ring imprisoning them. At one point, his hand remained stuck fast, and he couldn't pull any more. His skin burned and the pressure was almost unbearable. Weeping, he placed the sole of his boot against the thick table leg and, grasping his manacled wrist with his free hand, gave one final tug that propelled him backwards onto the sacks behind him. He spat out the napkin and, sobbing loudly, held up his hand to examine it, but with the windows closed, there wasn't enough light to see. He drew back the bolt on the street door and went outside where the late-afternoon sky was tinged with orange. His thumb was so thick with blood that he couldn't tell how bad the wound was. He went back inside and made straight for the barrel of water. He removed the cork and allowed the water to run freely over the wound. He drank some of the water too, then put the cork back. A strip of wrinkled skin was hanging loose from his thumb. The iron ring had cut him to the bone. He pressed his wounded hand to his chest and, clutching it with his other hand, wept out of pain and rage.

He carefully placed the strip of skin over the bone and smoothed it out as best he could to cover the wound. He then wrapped his hand in the napkin and, with the help of his teeth, tied a knot. The cloth immediately turned red with blood.

Before going out into the street again, he put two chorizos in his knapsack, along with a knife, some matches, a bottle of water and another of wine. He calculated that he still had two or three hours of daylight left. A trail of hoofprints and narrow wheel tracks led out of the village along the road by which he had entered. He adjusted the straps on his knapsack, pressed his wounded hand to his chest and began to run.

*   *   *

It was almost dark when he spotted the donkey trotting slowly southwards along a straight road flanked by ditches. The sole of the boy's boot had now come completely loose, and for some time he had been half-running, half-walking, with the front part of the sole flopping about like a black tongue. Now and then, some grit got into the boot, but he only stopped to empty it out when bothered by something really sharp. As he closed on his objective, he slowed down and kept to the side of the road, thinking that he could at least throw himself into one of the ditches if the cripple were to sense his presence and look back. When he was about a hundred yards away, he got a clear view of the cripple's makeshift wagon. He had made a kind of horse collar from a length of rope, one end of which he had tied to the plank to be used much like the reins on a yoke of oxen. He was beating the donkey with a stick as the ramshackle buggy skimmed clumsily over the ground. The donkey was once again laden with four panniers, two of which, the boy noticed, contained his water flasks. The only possible way this could have happened was for the cripple — no longer strapped to his plank, but resting all his weight on the stumps of his knees — somehow to have removed the flasks from the donkey's back, put new panniers on and lifted the water flasks into the panniers.

The cripple must be a very greedy man, the boy thought, to undertake a journey like that just for a reward, and this again made him wonder what price the bailiff had put on his head.

With only a few yards left before he caught up with them, the boy took even more care not to be seen. When he felt sure he could not possibly miss, he bent down, picked up a sharp stone about the size of a large potato and aimed it at the cripple's head. However, the stone whizzed past its intended target and struck the donkey squarely on the rump, causing the donkey, entirely out of character, to buck and bray furiously. It reached round to lick its wounded haunch and kicked wildly in all directions, one of those kicks striking the cripple on the forehead, rendering him unconscious. The donkey then began to trot aimlessly down the road, as if its load were as light as a feather, dragging the cripple's inert body, still strapped to the plank, from one side of the road to the other. The man's head bounced limply over the stones. Then the donkey calmed down slightly, turned and galloped back towards the boy, slowing its pace as it got nearer and stopping just short of the boy's feet. Stunned by the violence of what he'd just seen, the boy stared at the donkey as if he had tamed a fierce bull through the sheer power of thought. He held out his hand and the donkey approached meekly and sniffed his fingers. The edges of the plank had made ruts in the surface of the dirt road, marks blurred by the cripple's slewing body. The boy slid his hand under the donkey's jaw and stroked the loose skin. The donkey kept snorting like an angry child until it had fully recovered from the pain inflicted by that stone.

For a while, as night closed in on him, the boy stayed where he was, his arms around the donkey's head. He was resting, enjoying a silence broken only by the sound of the donkey's tail flicking away the horseflies, and letting time pass until he could summon up the courage to find out if the man was alive or dead. The donkey shook its head, and the coarse tuft of hair between its ears grazed the boy's face. Then the boy stepped away from the donkey and, as if it were something he had done time and again, walked determinedly round to the rear of the donkey to inspect the apparently lifeless body of his betrayer. He pressed one ear to the man's mouth and established that he was, in fact, still breathing. He felt the man's jacket and, in the inside pocket, found a tobacco pouch, a lighter and a folded piece of paper. He opened this out and held it up to the fading light. He couldn't make out the smaller lettering, but could read the large letters announcing his disappearance. A reward of twenty-five *monedas* was offered to anyone providing reliable information as to his whereabouts. He folded up the piece of paper again and put it back where he had found it.

He cut the ropes binding plank to donkey and gave the donkey a slap on the rump, thus permanently sundering that unlikely centaur. The donkey moved slightly to one side, leaving the man lying on the ground, the plank still strapped to his thighs, its greasy and now motionless ball bearings gazing up at the sky. The mark left by the donkey's hoof was imprinted on the man's forehead like a red letter U, and a jagged line of blood leaked from the wound made by one of the nails in the shoe. The boy was shaken both by the violence of the scene and by the recurring thought that this man had been intending to hand him over to his executioner. He gave the cripple a kick in the ribs that provoked a somnolent moan and sent the man rolling over the stones, his half-open mouth pressed into the dirt, on which a red spot of blood appeared.

The boy looked around him, recognised a few landmarks and reckoned that they must already be quite close to the sluice and the aqueduct. In his pursuit of the cripple, his one intention had been to stop him in his tracks, then abandon him on the road and continue on alone with the donkey and the water to find the goatherd. Now, with that large body lying at his feet, he had to reconsider his options. He knew that leaving him there meant condemning him to die within a matter of days beneath the hammering sun. Taking him with them would only slow them down and, even if the man were to forswear any further attempts at betrayal, he would clearly be a source of problems when they met up with the goatherd again. He considered dragging him back to the village and leaving him there safe among his provisions, but if he did that, he would definitely arrive too late to save the goatherd.

With his thumb throbbing under the napkin and his feet rubbed raw, the boy tried to put these various options into some hierarchy of importance so as to reach the right and fair decision, one that would save one man and condemn another to certain death. His heart was with the goatherd, but it was the body of the cripple that lay bleeding at his feet and whose twisted image he would carry with him for the rest of his days. He knew that whatever he decided to do, he would be committing a mortal sin and this reminded him of the village priest in the pulpit: his yellowing chasuble, his admonishing finger, the curve of his belly, and his spit raining down on his parishioners. The publican and the pharisee, the wise man and the fool, the meek and the proud, the whore and the mother. The categories which, it seemed, defined God's purposes or their opposites. These sermons had never brought him any enlightenment. The hell awaiting him at the end of his days would not, he thought, be so very different from the suffering he had known while alive. The flaming pit, full of black souls, could as easily be the plain with its pack of villains.

The cripple lying at his feet appeared to be regaining consciousness, writhing formlessly about on his wooden mount and moaning glutinous words that failed to cohere into any known meaning, doubtless the dialect of the hell-hound that would greet him at the gates of Hades. He imagined the cripple's amputated legs lying among the bushes. He thought of the goatherd, of his father and, lastly, of the bailiff, and that final image fixed itself on his eyelids like the flash of an explosion. The man gave another groan, and the boy, hardening his heart, kicked him in the mouth, opening up another gap among his already rotten teeth and returning him to his previous position on the road. The boy felt the blood flowing through his veins, felt it burning him inside. His scalp was pricking and his boots were full of grit. He looked about him, perhaps in search of witnesses or help, but found nothing and no one. Only the remains of an abandoned water tank a few yards from the road. For a second, he considered dragging the cripple over there and throwing him in so that no one would find him or so that he would bake to death the following day. He could drag his naked body over the rocks, tie his hands to the metal tubes that emerged out of the ground near the tank, harness him to the donkey and tear him limb from limb. Or he could take him with them, heal his wounds and ask his forgiveness. Then the man gave another distant groan, and the boy looked down at him. He took two steps back and dealt him another kick in the face, this time breaking his nose. Such was his torment and anguish.

9

He urged on the donkey, even though he knew this would have no effect. He wanted to get away as fast as possible from the place where he had left the cripple. He struggled fruitlessly to justify what he had done. Something about just men and sinners or about a needle, a camel and the kingdom of God. He couldn't be sure whether he had condemned the man to certain death or not. Before leaving him, he had emptied out the contents of his knapsack next to the body. On the other hand, he had then made off with the donkey laden with the two bottles of water and the food that the cripple had provided for his journey in search of the bailiff. Perhaps the road was better used than he imagined, and the following morning, the man would be safely stowed on some merchant's wagon, among sacks of dried chestnuts and apricots.

It was still dark when he spotted the ragged silhouette of the castle. The half-moon bathed the ruins in a watery blue wash. As he approached, he could make out the pile of bodies on one side and hear the clink of a bell from some goat already awake. The sound cheered him because, ever since he had left the castle the night before, there had been a kind of knot in the pit of his stomach: the idea that, when he returned, the goatherd would not be there. The tinkling bell did not, of course, come from the goatherd, but at least it was better than absolute silence. He dug his heels into the donkey and encouraged it to make haste by jiggling back and forth in the saddle. When they got closer to the dead goats, he heard the monotonous buzz of thousands of flies which he could not see, but which he imagined like a great black cloud hanging over that mound of death. Even though the wind wasn't blowing in his direction, he still had to cover his mouth against the pestilential smell so as not to vomit. A few yards from the wall, he jumped down from the donkey and hurried to the place where he had left the goatherd, but more urgent than checking on him was finding the saucepan and putting some water on to boil. The goatherd's possessions were there, but his 'bed' was empty. The boy squatted down next to the blanket and ran his hand over it just to confirm what his eyes were seeing. All his tension evaporated and he felt it rise up to join the warm, ascending current of air given off by the wall. He sat down beside the blanket and, resting his elbows on his knees, covered his face with his hands and wept. His childish flight, the searing sun, the bleak, indifferent plain. He sensed the immutability of his surroundings, the same inertness in everything he could touch or see and, for the first time since he had run away, he felt afraid of dying. The idea of carrying on alone terrified him, and the image flashed into his mind of his house beside the railway track and the silo. He could decide to go back. He could abandon his desperate struggle against nature and against men and return home. Well, if not home exactly, at least to some kind of shelter. He would return in a far worse state than when he left. He wasn't the prodigal son. He had rejected his family and would have to accept whatever verdict they passed on him. He was thinking these thoughts because the plain had worn him down in a way he could never have imagined while living safe beneath a roof. He found this state of utter helplessness exhausting and, at such moments, would gladly have exchanged even the most precious part of his being to enjoy a little peace or simply to be able to satisfy his most basic needs quietly and naturally. These other things: protecting himself from the sun, wringing from the earth every last drop of water, inflicting pain on himself, liberating himself from slavery, deciding on other people's lives, none of these things were appropriate to his still-expanding brain, his still-growing bones, his supple limbs, his physical frame on the verge of becoming something larger and more angular. He imagined the goatherd's lifeless body being dragged along behind the bailiff's motorbike and the bailiff's deputies on horseback, laughing.

In the darkness, he cupped his face in his hands. A small, warm place in which to hide away. A tiny room in which he would be spared the sight of that eternal, futile plain stretching away beneath him. In this seclusion, he found one dirty hand and one hand wrapped in a dusty napkin, the bundle concealing his torn and throbbing thumb. No, even there he could find no rest.

'Get up, boy.'

The goatherd's quavering voice and his bony hand on his shoulder. The boy sprang to his feet and, without even looking at the goatherd, he flung his arms about his frail body. He pressed his face into the old man's rags so as to become one with him, to enter the tranquil room his own hands had denied him. It was the first time he had been so close to someone without trying to fight him off. The first time he had been skin to skin with someone and allowed all the humours and substances of his being to flow forth from his pores. The goatherd welcomed him without a word, as if he were welcoming a pilgrim or an exile. The boy embraced him so tightly that the goatherd cried out: 'Mind my ribs,' and immediately the knot dissolved and they separated. There was no embarrassment, just the discreet distance required by the laws of that land and that time. The seed, however, had been sown.

★   ★   ★

They boiled some water, and once the goatherd and the goats had drunk it, the old man and the boy ate the cripple's sausages right down to the strings and drank the cripple's wine, the old man taking long swallows and the boy trying unsuccessfully to conceal his grimaces. He drank because the goatherd drank and because he felt that, after his strange journey he was a different person: the boy who had risked his life to bring water back for a few goats and who had deliberately aimed a stone at a cripple's head. Then, when they had eaten and drunk their fill, the boy told the goatherd all about his adventure. The goatherd said:

'We have to find that man before the crows peck him to death.'

The boy felt all the old tension in his muscles descend on him from above, and his jaw tightened. He turned to the old man, unable to understand what he had just heard, but the goatherd did not return his look. The boy knew that what he had done was not good, but rather than being told to set off to help the man who had wanted to kill him, he had expected a pat on the back or a firm handshake, as a sign of approval or respect. The goatherd might not have been prepared to greet him like a hero or recognise the sacrifice he had made, but he should certainly not oblige him to put his head back in the lion's mouth. He studied the goatherd's hands, remembered his swollen eyelids and the triangular marks left on his back by the riding whip. The old man was clearly not going to be the one to hand him the key to the world of adults, that world in which brutality was meted out for reasons of greed or lust. He himself had been guilty of meting out violence, exactly as he had seen those around him do, and now he was demanding his share of impunity. The elements had pushed him far beyond what he knew and didn't know about life. It had taken him to the very edge of death and there, in the midst of that camp of horrors, he had raised his sword rather than proffered his neck. He felt he had drunk of the blood that transforms boys into warriors and men into invulnerable beings. The old man should, he thought, have marched him through the victory arch, crowned with laurels by a slave.

'That crippled bastard chained me up and then ran off to tell the bailiff.'

'He, too, is a child of God.'

'That 'child of God' wants us dead.'

* * *

They woke before dawn and set off along the towpath. The old man riding the donkey, his head drooping, and the boy leading the way, with a stick in one hand and the halter in the other. Since the dog was no longer with them, the boy was the one who had to keep the goats moving whenever they stopped to graze.

While they walked, the boy kept thinking about the cripple. The image of that pile of flesh and bones he had left lying in the dust returned to him over and over. Would he still be there? Would he have been able to right himself and set his wheels on the road? As he recalled, the plank had very wide axles, which was good when it came to surviving potholes, but a problem should he fall over. The boy didn't know what he would feel when he saw him. The last time they had met, they were still *compadres*. Then came his captivity, the theft of the donkey, the cripple's flight, the stone aimed at the cripple's head, the kicks he had dealt him before abandoning him to his fate, and since then there had been no chance to explain or clarify anything.

As it grew light, they were able to make out the mountains in the distance. The plain was like a sea that ended abruptly at the foot of those northern slopes, but, at that moment, they were merely a watery illusion. A boundary, a goal, a reminder that a place might exist where one could breathe more easily. Those misty mountains held a magnetic attraction for him. He imagined himself reaching the end of the plain and entering those foothills. The goatherd, the goats and the donkey were with him. Together they entered via a fold in the hills and ascended to a high plateau, walking along a path that wound through unfamiliar trees. The path was raised up above wooded slopes and followed the comings and goings of shady gullies. Every now and then, they would stop to rest and he would amuse himself by making little boats from the bark fallen from tall pine trees. Higher up, in the meadows, they would find lodging in a stone shelter with a heather roof. In his dream, the herd of goats had grown in size and was scattered over the length and breadth of a green and fragrant plateau. Towards the north, the mountains grew steadily higher. They rose above the woods and scrub like stone nipples. Higher still were the white peaks, where the eternal snows filled crevices that appeared to have been gouged out by some giant. To the south, a dramatic overhang provided a balcony from which they could survey the plain. The same plain that they were now crossing, their eyes bruised by the pitiless hammer of the sun's rays. In the evenings, after they had milked the goats and the old man was settled comfortably on his blanket, they would sit on the overhang and contemplate the plain, which would seem to them a vague and distant place. From the vantage point of their abundance, they would summon the angels and archangels to carry to their village the rain that would restore fertility to the wheatfields. The men and their families would return and move back into their old houses, and the silo would once again be full. They would all be awash with money, the bailiff would receive his taxes, and no one would ever again recall the boy who disappeared.

They reached the sluice at an hour when the sun was at its most crushing. The boy helped the old man off the donkey and settled him down against a hollow ash tree. They drank some of the warm water they had boiled the previous night. The boy said to the old man:

'We have no food.'

'You'll have to go and find some.'

'Why did we leave the salted meat back at the castle?'

'It wasn't properly cured yet.'

'It might have finished curing during the journey.'

Unaccustomed to having to explain himself, the goatherd shot the boy an irritated glance.

'I didn't realise we would have to leave the castle so soon.'

'We could have stayed longer if you'd wanted to.'

The old man raised his head, the way a flower on a dungheap might raise its head. He stared stonily at the boy, who immediately lowered his grubby chin onto his chest.

The goatherd then ordered him to dig up some liquorice root, pointing to the places where it would be easiest to find. With head still lowered, the boy took the knife from the old man's pouch and walked over to a low bank near the aqueduct. At that time of year, he assumed he would have to dig down deep to find anything fresh to chew on.

He returned with his sleeves all smeared with earth and holding a few twisted roots. Sitting down next to the old man, he cut the roots into pencil-length pieces and peeled the tips of two of them. The man began chewing on his, but immediately had to stop because even his jaw hurt him.

'Are you in a lot of pain?'

'Yes.'

'Is there anything I can do?'

'You'll have to clean my wounds.'

The boy pulled the old man's body away from the tree trunk, carefully removed his jacket and put it to one side. Then he unbuttoned the man's shirt, leaving his chest bare. Fortunately, none of the wounds were open or suppurating, but the goatherd was in an extremely weakened state. Following the old man's instructions, the boy dipped a piece of cloth in water and, taking enormous care, slowly drew it along the weals on his chest. The goatherd didn't complain at all; he merely gritted his teeth and closed his eyes when the boy pressed too hard. The boy wondered if the old man had broken something or was simply too old to withstand a beating like that. He remembered the first time he'd seen him wrapped up in his blanket in the middle of the night and how long it had taken him just to sit up. He realised then that before the goatherd had met him, his life had probably been limited to herding the goats from one grazing area to another, but never covering any great distances. Why had he been so generous in his help? Why had he tested his body to the limit by undertaking that brutal journey? Why had he not handed him over to the bailiff at the castle? His silence had cost him a large part of his herd and placed him at death's door.

He had the goatherd lie down on his side in the shade of the ash tree. Up until then, he had only cleaned the wounds on the old man's chest and sides; however, his back was criss-crossed by five long brown weals. The grimy fabric of his shirt had become stuck to his skin beneath a crust of dried blood. The boy told the goatherd what he could see, and the goatherd told him how to proceed. First, he poured bowlfuls of water onto the goatherd's back to soften the dried blood and allow him to unstick the cloth from the wounds without causing them to open up. He repeated this operation several times until, with extreme care, he began to peel the cloth away. When he had removed the whole shirt, he spread it out as best he could on the ground so that the old man could see on it the negative image of his back. The image troubled the old man even more than the pain from the wounds themselves, and he sat for a while staring at this image of his martyrdom. Then he suddenly lost interest and lay down again so that the boy could continue his work. Most of the wounds were swollen in places or had whitish pustules on them, signs of infection. The boy described these to the old man and, at that moment, the old man knew that without any alcohol to disinfect them, without any rest, it would be the infection and not his arthritis that would finish him off.

'When I die, bury me as best you can, and put a cross on my grave, even if it's only a cross made of stones.'

The boy stopped cleaning the wounds.

'You're not going to die.'

'Of course I am. Will you put a cross on my grave?'

The view the boy had of the plain from that wretched bit of shade turned watery. The slightly undulating ground, the aqueduct and the mountains they were heading for all grew blurred.

'Will you put a cross on my grave?'

'Yes.'

★ ★ ★

They waited drowsily for the heat to abate, then set off again, the boy having draped the jacket over the old man's shoulders. A couple of hours later, they came within sight of the water tank, but there was no sign of the cripple. The boy thought that perhaps he had managed to drag himself into the shade. They walked on until they had a clearer view of the area, but still no trace. The boy let go of the halter and ran down to the tank. The cripple wasn't inside nor was he leaning against one of the crumbling pillars of the aqueduct. The boy scoured the road in search of the exact spot where he had left the man and soon found some small telltale bloodstains and, a little further on, the sharp stone with which he had hit the donkey. He also found the hoofprints of at least two horses and noticed the scuffed-up earth on the embankment. Following those hoofprints, he saw that the horses had gone their separate ways, one to the north and the other to the south. Beside the road, he found a pile of fresh dung. Then the goatherd and the goats arrived.

'He's gone,' the boy said, and with a lift of his chin indicated the pile of dung.

★　★　★

They spent the night in the tank. There was a gap in one side through which the boy had helped the old man to enter. The tank was scalding hot, giving back the heat it had absorbed during the day, but it was preferable

180

to lying on the stony ground outside. They dined on goat's milk and, chewing on the roots the boy had dug up that morning, the old man fell asleep. He had barely spoken during the day and, apart from when the boy had been cleaning his wounds, hadn't uttered a single word of complaint. At night, though, it was different. Almost as soon as he fell asleep, the old man began to moan and didn't stop until near dawn. The boy witnessed his delirium with a mixture of sympathy and torpor. He heard the first moans while he was still gazing up at the whitish glow of the night, waiting for sleep to come. He sat up and looked across at the old man, who was tossing and turning on his blanket. With every movement, his bones juddered on the hard floor of the tank, like a dice tumbling over marble, bringing new pain. At one point, in the crescent moon's bluish light, he noticed that the old man's eyelids were wet with tears that trickled down over his skeletal cheek-bones. Shortly before dawn, the delirium ceased and only then did the boy go to sleep. A few moments later, at first light, he felt the old man's hand shaking his shoulder.

'We fell asleep. We have to go.'

He had only slept for about a quarter of an hour, but when he sat up, he felt as if he had spent the whole night resting on a good wool mattress. He thought about the old man, about his moans and his tears, and for a while he wasn't sure whether that had really happened or if he had dreamed it. He cupped one hand and filled it with water from the flask, then splashed his face with it before standing up to peer over the wall of the tank. The morning breeze made his damp skin feel still cooler, and for a moment, he felt as if he were walking up a hill with the wind from a new valley beyond coming to meet him. A non-existent valley unless one considered that endless plain to be the bottom of something bounded by the mountains to the north and by some other unknown mountain range to the south.

'Hurry up, boy.'

The boy collected together their few belongings, rolled up the old man's blanket and helped him onto the donkey. He rounded up the goats and they went back to the road. Once there, they both simultaneously glanced to right and left, as if not having found the cripple had left them with nothing to do. The old man scratched his beard, then indicated with a nod of his head that they should go north, and they set off. Four hours later, they reached the oak wood near the deserted village and, without a word being exchanged, plunged into it.

When the old man was comfortably installed next to an oak, he instructed the boy to make a corral out of a rough circle of trees, filling up any gaps between the gnarled trunks with fallen branches. Once the goats were safely inside, the boy unloaded the donkey and sat down with the goatherd, awaiting new orders.

'We have to leave.'

'We've only just arrived.'

'I mean we have to leave the plain.'

'You can stay. I'm the one the bailiff's looking for.'

'Look at me.'

The goatherd opened his jacket to reveal his body.

'I have my own scores to settle with that man.'

His lacerated body made it clear enough what those scores were, although it did not even occur to the boy to ask if the old man was referring to the recent beating he had received or to some earlier offence. In such a sparsely populated area, it was quite likely, he thought, that the two men's paths would already have crossed.

The old man told him that they would escape into the mountains to the north, because it would be easier to hide there and he was sure that the bailiff would not take his pursuit of them into territory so far outside his jurisdiction. He explained, too, that it was an area where water could be found all year round and that, with luck, even the goats might improve. The boy listened in silence, nodding his agreement.

The journey would be long and dangerous and it was important that they start as soon as possible. He also said that they would have to travel at night so as to avoid meeting other people. They would need all the food they could lay their hands on.

They agreed that the boy would go down to the inn to see how the land lay. If the cripple wasn't there, he would come back to the wood and they would go down to the inn together, take the food and continue on their way north.

'And what if the cripple is there?'

'Then you'll come back here and we'll think of another plan.'

10

So as to avoid the path, the boy decided to take the same route across the fields as he had two nights before. The old man watched him go and, initially, heard the loose sole of his boot flapping on the ground, carving a leaf-free trail of its own. Before the boy left the shade of the trees, he turned and met the goatherd's eyes, but neither he nor the old man could possibly imagine the brutal nature of what awaited them.

Once out of the woods, the boy crawled the first few yards, his knapsack clasped to his side, until he had reached a point where he had a fairly clear view of the village. He stayed there for a while, watching for any signs of life. He would have preferred to spend more time scrutinising each of those houses in turn, but the memory of his last bout of sunstroke began to beat like a pulse on the back of his neck, and he decided to carry on. Head down, walking briskly, almost running, he got as far as the cemetery, but this time he didn't stop there. He continued running, not in a straight line, but in an arc so as to take early advantage of the church as a screen between him and the inn. During all that time, he kept his knapsack clutched to him and his eyes permanently trained on the village. When he reached the church, the muscles in his neck were stiff with tension and the base of his skull ached. He leaned his back against the wall and slid down it, causing bits of whitewash to flake off. A microscopic snowstorm in the desert. The sun was almost immediately overhead now and, for a moment, he was tempted to wait there until the sun had proceeded on its way and provided him with a little shade from the building. From where he was, he could see the grey, earthy colours of the oak trees and he thought of the old man leaning against the trunk where he had left him only shortly before. He recalled the goatherd opening his jacket to show him his bruised torso, the wounds in his sides and the suppurating scar between his ribs similar to the wound Christ must have had on the cross. He had a sudden vision of the old man, which emerged from some unknown place inside him and which, in the middle of that godforsaken wasteland, filled him with cold fear. The field he had just crossed was like the image of some deeply painful experience. For the first time since he had met the goatherd, he felt he was losing touch with the one solid piece of ground that had sustained him in the midst of that sea of shifting sand. He wanted to go back to the oak wood and even placed his hands on the ground and made as if to move away from the wall. Then he stopped, because there was more salvation in the cripple's cured meats than there was in his fear that he would never see the goatherd again.

Keeping close to the wall, he walked round the church and concerned himself solely with watching the far end of the village where the inn was located. He did not expect to see many signs of life from a man as badly disabled as the cripple. At most, an open shutter or a little smoke from the chimney. He felt a grumbling in his intestines, as if someone inside him were boiling a pot full of rubber bands. During the time he had been standing there, the shade from the acacia tree next to the porch had reached as far as a large clump of agaves at the entrance to the village. Hunched down and still without taking his eyes off the inn, he made his way over to that clump and again waited. This was the last bit of shelter before he would be forced out into the open. He once more weighed up his options and, although he had seen nothing to indicate that the cripple was in the village, the fear of another encounter with him neverthe-less gnawed at him. Around him, the stems of the agave flowers stood like dead spears, their papery blooms like withered bouquets. He rubbed his face with his hands, grimacing and screwing up his eyes. His wounds had grown dry with salt and fear.

For a long time, he was gripped by doubts, in a state of the most terrible tension. Not even the sun beating down on his head could get him to move. Faced by the open space between him and the inn, he was somehow hoping that his legs would start walking of their own volition, but this didn't happen until the headache brought on by the sun grew unbearable. Then he crawled out from behind the agaves and very gradually straightened up and began to run unobserved towards the backs of the empty houses.

He reached the low wall of a corral and lay down, listening and watching for any sound or movement. He had completely blanked out the few moments he had remained in full view. His heart was pounding so hard that he could feel his pulse in his neck, his temples and his groin. His head was throbbing and, looking back at the church and beyond that, at the oak wood, he realised that what was holding him there was the fear of reaching a point of no return: the place where he was now, far from the shade of the oak trees, far from the many escape routes along the perimeter of the wood, far from the old man's poor bruised arms. Enemy territory with no soldiers visible, but full of shadows and dark corners.

He sat down by the wall and shook his head, trying to shake off his inertia. He tried taking some deep breaths, and his mind, as if by magic, emptied of all the things that had been paralysing it. He again felt that grumbling in his stomach, and the feeling of tightness and pressure in his brain eased. He turned round and peered over the corral wall, which was immediately adjacent to a house with its roof caved in. The bare bones of wicker chairs with no seats and no backs, contorted piles of chicken wire resembling souls in torment or skeletons made of smoke, piles of rubble consisting of roof tiles and the mud from the adobe washed out by the rain and deposited at the foot of the thick house walls. A breeze blew through the building, from the front to the courtyard at the back, setting the cobwebs trembling. He crouched down and, keeping close to the wall, he began heading north along the backs of the houses, slipping like a shadow in and out of each crumbling cavity, until he reached the last house before the inn. There he found a final refuge in the doorway, where he waited in silence, just in case he heard some sound from the cripple. He waited for as long as seemed prudent, until he felt sure that the man was not inside. Although maybe it was so quiet because the cripple was asleep either there or in the shade of the vine trellis covering the façade. Only the vague memory of those sausages and cured meats tempted him to throw caution to the wind and enter the house like a policeman or a thief, but this was a big risk to take with someone like the cripple. Not because of the cripple himself, but because of whoever had brought him back. Into the boy's head came that final image of the man lying in the road. The drool, the blood, the mud. He ran his hand over his own forehead, as if expecting to find there the wound the donkey had inflicted on the cripple when provoked by that stone. Then he looked around him and, abandoning the safety of the doorway, crept over to the back window of the inn. He was protected there by shutters identical to those at the front. Green metal shutters with a diamond pattern of perforations in the centre of each leaf. He pulled the shutters slightly open, then waited, his ear on a level with the window ledge. After a while, he stood up and peered in. He felt cool air coming from inside and allowed that air to lick the tight skin on his face. The air smelled of damp flax and stillness, of the crumbling whitewash and mud from the adobe that had accumulated around the skirting boards. He stayed in that position for a while, as if he had plunged his face into a clear cool stream. In other circumstances, that breeze would have ruffled his hair, but after so many days without washing, his hair was thick and matted. Behind the shutters were two metal-framed glass windows. The few unbroken panes of glass were covered in grime and dust. Through the gap in the shutters he could see into the dim interior of the room. The first thing he noticed were the pinpricks of light on the floor from the diamond-shaped pattern on the shutters. When his eyes had grown accustomed to the dark, he could make out the table and the iron bar from which hung the various cured meats. His mouth filled with saliva and he felt a pain in his stomach as if someone were gripping his intestines with pincers, and then, as if both will and fear had been simultaneously vanquished, he opened the shutters fully and climbed up onto the window ledge. From there, he pushed open the windows, allowing new light into the room and, from that moment, he had eyes only for the sausages, their skins pearled with oil, and the sides of ham dripping grease like some kind of porcine still. He jumped down, and the tile he landed on wobbled beneath him. The floor tiles, he noticed, bore a faded geometric design. There was a strange tension in the air that he hadn't noticed before. He glanced rapidly around the room and, seeing no one, fixed his gaze on the meat.

In three strides he had reached the opposite wall, grabbed the nearest chorizo and held it in front of him in his two hands like someone about to coil up a rope. He stuffed the red meat into his mouth, undeterred by the spiciness or by the nervous state of his stomach. He simply surrendered to the savage instinct that says: eat first and worry about getting ill later. He devoured the entire sausage, swallowing bits of it almost whole, and when he'd finished, he wiped his mouth on his sleeve, smearing it with grease and paprika.

While he was gulping down the last piece, he paused for a while, studying the metal bar, wanting something different to sink his teeth into. Standing on tiptoe, he sniffed the salami, but it smelled slightly off. He then sniffed a blood sausage and was seduced by its fragrance, almost imperceptible amongst all the other smells. He tugged at the string and bit into the sausage and, as he did so, he heard a noise which, at first, he interpreted as the sound of a tooth breaking. He touched his cheek, but, feeling no pain, he spun round, like someone suddenly aware of being watched. His eyes explored the most brightly lit areas first and then the darker ones, some of which were plunged in impenetrable gloom. He could see nothing. He carefully put the sausage down on the table and stood — legs apart, ready for action, ears cocked like a horse — in the middle of the rectangle of light flooding in through the window onto the tiled floor. He turned round very slowly and that was when he saw him.

He was lying inside the pantry located in one corner of the room, concealed behind a patterned curtain. The curtain did not quite reach the floor and underneath it he could see what appeared to be an elbow. He took shelter behind the table, waiting for something to happen. He kept his eyes fixed on that elbow, but saw not the slightest movement nor heard the slightest sound. At first, he thought the owner of the elbow, possibly the cripple, might be asleep, only to realise that no one in his right mind would choose to take a nap in such a place. Perhaps it was a drunk or someone, like him, who had come in search of those sausages or the wine in the earthenware pitcher. He looked around for something he could use to lift the curtain without having to get too close. He found a long pole with a kind of pincer at the end, like the one used by the shopkeeper in the village to reach the highest shelves. He picked it up and approached the pantry. When he was about six feet away, he reached out the pole and with the pincer end touched the curtain. However, he couldn't sustain the weight of the pole held at full length and one end dropped down, accidentally striking what must have been the head of the man behind the curtain. He again drew back and waited for some response, but nothing happened. The light coming in through the window by which he had entered seemed to lend volume to the air. Outside that block of light, in the spot where he could now see that elbow, and in all the other shadowy corners, unimaginable dangers lurked.

Trembling, he again reached out the pole to the curtain. This time he managed to pull it aside and immediately recognised the cripple's face. The wound was still there on the man's forehead, like a brand. In his efforts to reveal the whole body, he tugged so hard that the metal curtain rail came off at one end. Rail and curtain fell to the ground with a dull thud. The dust from floor and curtain flew up like pigeons startled by a passing horse, then dissolved into the darkness.

The cripple's naked body reminded him of a full wineskin, completely hairless and with scars like stitching on his rounded stumps. He went over to the body and with the tip of his boot touched the man's stomach, chest and shoulder, but there was no response. Bending down, he grabbed the man's chin and shook his head. He opened the man's eyelids and found only two blank spheres the colour of yellowing ivory. He walked backwards, his eyes still fixed on the man, until he collided with the wall, where he sat down.

He studied that formless body for a long time, wondering if he had been the one to kill him. After all, the last time he had seen him, that had been an option. True, he hadn't acted on that option and the cripple had only been unconscious, not dead, when he left him by the water tank. Given his physical limitations, however, and the inhospitable nature of the place, he could easily have died there. He stared hard at the man's chest to see if there was any sign of breathing, but there was nothing in him now that could fill his lungs. The boy struggled to understand what could have happened, but he only had room in his head for the idea of death. He had heard a lot about death, although usually only in the priest's sermons. The Egyptians dying in their thousands beneath the waters of the Red Sea, Herod massacring the innocents, or Jesus crucified on Golgotha. But this was quite different, and he didn't know what to do about it.

He spent a couple of hours contemplating the corpse, marvelling at its shapes and paralysed by the gravity of what he could see. During that time, the afternoon light softened and things in the room grew dimmer. And even though he had hardly slept the previous night, he did not succumb to sleep. While he was studying the cripple, he couldn't even thread two thoughts together, his mind entirely occupied with his contemplation of that strange sight. It would not have taken much for him to remember the hoofprints heading off in different directions from the water tank where he had left the cripple. And yet he didn't even notice the purple line around the cripple's neck, clearly left by a noose, nor did he ask himself why the body was naked. He didn't realise the danger he was in and remained in that stunned state until he heard something scratching at the door.

He leapt to his feet and stood with his back and the palms of his hands pressed against the wall. When he identified the noise as coming from an animal scratching at the wood, he relaxed. He went over to the door and opened it a crack. The goatherd's dog was gazing up at him, wagging its tail, its tongue lolling. He opened the door fully to welcome the dog, which jumped enthusiastically up at him. As he had done so often before, the boy bent down and scratched the dog under its chin. From that position, he could see the legs of a man sitting on the bench outside one of the windows and, realising who it was, he sprang back, intending to shut the door.

He had nearly succeeded when the boot of another man thrust itself in between door and door frame. The boy kept trying to push the door shut, but the boot stopped him. When he realised that he couldn't close the door, he ran towards the back of the house to make his escape through the window he had entered by. He saw the rectangle of light, the fading afternoon sun outside and, in the distance, the church. He tried to jump from the window and would have made it if the bailiff's man had not been waiting for him, having run round the house from the front. He was holding a double-barrelled Beretta shotgun with ivory inlay. The boy managed to draw back in time, only narrowly avoiding falling into the man's arms, but coming close enough to penetrate the alcoholic aura surrounding him. The same sickly smell he had so often smelled on his father when he came back from the bar at night. He barely had time to look at the man's face, and yet his image remained engraved on his memory: the gingerish hair, the sweaty, greying beard, the empty blue eyes and, above all, the tip of his greasy nose covered in a network of bulging blue veins.

He turned round, because although he had exhausted all escape routes, something inside him was nonetheless hoping that the ground would open up beneath him or that the walls might suddenly sprout new doors. Instead, what he found under the inn's fragile roof was the dapper, feline figure of the bailiff. The sight shook him to the marrow.

'Well, look who's here.'

The bailiff took off his hat and smoothed his hair.

'Have you seen this, Colorao?'

His deputy nodded, leaning his elbows on the window ledge, and he continued nodding as he examined the room. He gave the same degree of attention to the roof beams as to the cripple's naked body and, when he had inspected every corner of the room, he gestured to the bailiff, indicating the sausages hanging from the bar. Still without taking his eyes off the boy, the bailiff grabbed a sausage and threw it to his colleague. The man missed, and the sausage struck one of the panes of glass and fell to the floor. Resting his belly on the window ledge, the man stretched down to reach the sausage. He picked it up, wiped off any bits of glass with his sleeve, then walked away, chewing on the tough meat.

The bailiff also scanned the room as if it were a place full of memories for him, then went to the back window. Stepping over the broken glass on the floor, he gazed out at the plain. Then, as if a storm were approaching, he reached for the shutters, pulled them to and put the catch on. The dog had come into the house and was lying at the boy's feet, sniffing at the puddle that had formed there.

Someone tapped on the shutters and the bailiff opened them again.

'Any chance there might be something in there to drink, boss?'

The bailiff's deputy again leaned on the ledge while the bailiff searched the room. The deputy looked the boy up and down, as if imagining what was about to happen to him. The bailiff returned and handed him a half-gallon flask of wine.

'Now go away and don't bother me again.'

The deputy uncorked the flask and tossed the cork into the room. Hooking two fingers round the wicker handle, he rested the flask on his forearm, which he then lifted to his lips before taking a long, long drink. The bailiff said tetchily:

'Don't overdo the wine, all right? You'll have work to do in the morning.'

The deputy lowered the flask and gave the bailiff a leering grin, his eyes bleary and heavy-lidded. Staring at some vague point in the room, he belched loudly, then turned and left.

'Useless bloody drunk,' muttered the bailiff, leaning out over the ledge to close the shutters again. When he had drawn the bolt, he pushed at the shutters just to make sure they were securely closed. He looked through the slats of one of them, then turned round, the broken glass again crunching beneath his boots. From there, he studied the boy from head to toe, as if regarding some tasty morsel.

'Don't be afraid, boy. Nothing's going to happen to you.'

The bailiff smiled and added: 'Nothing new anyway.'

Very slowly, he crossed the room and when he reached the boy's side, he bent down, picked up the dog's lead, led the dog over to the door and shut him outside. Before closing the door again, he saw his deputy meandering down the street towards the entrance to the village. In one hand, he was holding his shotgun and, in the other, the flask from which he took long, regular draughts. The bailiff closed the shutters on the front of the house too, and the room was left in darkness. A few grim seconds passed during which all the boy could hear was the man moving about somewhere in the room. Then the bailiff flicked on his lighter and, with it, lit a large tallow candle that the boy hadn't noticed before. Then he walked around the room, picking up whatever bits of food he fancied — smoked pork, chorizo and ham as well as the bottle of olive oil. He poured some wine from the large pitcher into a smaller earthenware jug and placed it on the table. When he went over to the pantry, he had to kick one of the cripple's arms out of the way in order to get a tin plate and a glass from a shelf. He also helped himself to a handful of breadsticks from a jar. When he had everything he needed, he sat down and started to eat as if he were entirely alone. He cut slices of sausage to eat along with the breadsticks, occasionally adding a drizzle of olive oil.

While the man was eating, the boy remained standing, head bowed. His wet boots, his grimy skin, the smell of the food, an end to his bold adventure. He took for granted the coming nightmare and didn't cry, because he had been here dozens of times before. It was a matter of indifference to him now whether the bailiff killed him or took him back to the village. His fate was decided, as was that of the goatherd.

By the time the man had finished eating, the pinprick pattern of light from the shutters had faded completely. He pushed away what remained of his food with one arm, then got up. He grabbed a handful of walnuts from a sack leaning against one of the walls and deposited them on the part of the table he had just cleared. He sat down again and cracked them open, sticking the point of his knife into the base of each nut and turning it until the shell split in two. Then, despite his large fingers, he managed to scoop the kernels out almost whole and put them in a bowl. All this time, the boy stood motionless. The puddle at his feet had seeped into the grouting around the tiles, but his trouser legs were still wet and he could feel a slight numbness in his calf muscles.

'It's important to do things properly.'

The bailiff made this remark while holding one half of a nutshell in each hand. Then holding each half between two fingers, he put them together so that they fitted perfectly like a brain with four hemispheres.

'And you haven't.'

The boy continued staring at the wall,

transfixed by the magnetic presence of the bailiff and by his memories of him. Those memories swam around like catfish at the bottom of a well of black water.

'How often have I told you not to tell anyone else about us?'

'I haven't said anything to anyone.'

The boy lifted his head slightly, and there was a note of almost childish complaint in his voice.

'What about the goatherd?'

The bailiff took a bite out of a walnut, then returned it to the bowl. The boy said nothing, trying as best he could to play a role that was no longer his.

'I don't know what you're talking about.'

'I mean the old man you've been travelling with these last few days. Or do you expect me to believe that you got here all on your own?'

Then the boy's legs gave way beneath him and he sank to the floor, feeling utterly helpless, even more helpless than when his father had taken him to that man's house for the first time and left him there, at the mercy of his desires. He shrank in on himself, as if trying to unite two wetnesses, the damp floor and his own moist eyes. The liturgy, so often repeated, was starting all over again: the bailiff sitting down, placing one foot on his knee in order to untie the laces on his boots, which he then picked up by the heels and placed neatly on the floor. Pushing the chair to one side and getting to his feet in order to unbutton his shirt. Walking over to him, bare-chested.

'Stand up.'

The boy obeyed and stood before him, head still bowed.

'Raise your head.'

The boy did not move, head down, fists and toes clenched.

'I'm ordering you to look at me.'

Up until then, the boy had managed not to cry, but now he suddenly let out a sob.

With one hand, the bailiff smoothed the boy's matted hair. He stroked his neck and ran the back of his fingers gently over the boy's wet cheeks. The man then raised his fingers to his lips and tasted the mixture of salt and soot and tears.

'Look at me.'

The bailiff tried to force the boy to lift his head, but again, the boy resisted.

'Okay if that's how you want it.'

He then propelled him towards the table and ordered him to place his hands wide apart on the wooden tabletop. Tears spilled forth from the boy's swollen eyes and rolled grimily down his cheeks into the bowl of walnuts.

The candle, which, by now, had almost

burned down to nothing, cast harsh shadows of their bodies onto walls and ceiling. Behind him, the boy heard rhythmic movements and the bailiff's heavy breathing.

Suddenly, the candle went out, and the man gave a snort of annoyance. In the dark, he fumbled around in the corner where he had found the candle, but, failing to find what he wanted, he went over to the pantry. He stepped over the cripple's dead body and picked up the fallen curtain. He tore a couple of strips from it and went back to the table, twisting them in his fingers. He poured some olive oil onto his plate and arranged the two strips of cloth to form a cross, making sure these were thoroughly soaked in oil. Then, like someone twirling a moustache, he twisted the ends so that they stood upright to form four points. He felt for his lighter in his jacket pocket, flicked it on and held the flame to the bits of cloth until four small crackling flames appeared. The new light lit up the room, and the boy could see the bailiff's boots next to his chair, his shirt draped over the back. The man again positioned himself behind the boy and was just about to start again, when someone knocked at the door.

'Bloody hell, Colorao! Didn't I tell you to leave me in peace? What the fuck do you want now?'

The bailiff's voice echoed around the room as he turned his head towards the door. The door creaked very slowly open and the breeze from the street made the flames flicker. Standing on the threshold, holding the deputy's shotgun, the goatherd cut a faintly ridiculous figure: his bent back, his baggy trousers and his face gaunt from exhaustion and years of hardship. He was so weak he could hardly stand and had to lean against the door frame so as not to fall over. He was breathing hard.

'Go away, old man.'

The goatherd did not move, the eyes of the double-barrelled shotgun fixed on the bailiff's head. He tried to say something, but choked and coughed. Without lowering the shotgun, he spat out a bloody gob of spit, then said:

'Come here, boy.'

With the bailiff's hand still grasping his shoulder, the boy did not move.

'You'd better drop the shotgun, old man, or you're going to regret it for what little remains of your life.'

'Lie down on the ground, boy, and cover your ears.'

The goatherd's voice sounded as firm as the handshake of a strong young man. It had a stone-hard quality that came from some hitherto unknown place inside the old man, a voice completely out of keeping with the spectral figure saying the words. An Angel of Fire come to break down walls. The boy obeyed that second order and very slowly shrank back, leaving the bailiff standing, his hand poised like a pincer where the boy's shoulder had been. The bailiff was paralysed not by fear, but by astonishment.

'You haven't got the balls, goatherd.'

'Don't look, boy.'

★ ★ ★

A noise, cavernous and absolute, as if emerging from the end of a long tube. A buzzing in his skull and a deafness that would take days to disappear entirely. Many of the pigeons who soiled the filthy houses with their excrement escaped through the sunken roofs and flew off wildly in all directions. The boy felt the body fall at his side as the displaced air pressed up against him. The tiled floor received the man's body and the boy felt the vibration. In his bewilderment, he heard the last sound the bailiff made, that of his skull hitting the ground. Like a very ripe pumpkin. The thick skin that yields only to the machete or the bullet, its filling of dense, tightly packed, floury pulp spilling out. A single blow and it was all over.

When the boy finally opened his eyes, the goatherd had come into the room and was leaning against the table. The boy didn't know how long he had kept his eyes closed. He could feel liquid coming out of his ears. A small plume of smoke was still issuing forth from the barrel of the shotgun and a sulphurous cloud was rising up into the gaps between the roof beams. Next to him lay an incoherent, lifeless heap of bones and muscles. The warmth of that body close to his. The goatherd's voice reaching him as if in a paraffin-drenched dream, A scream opening its way through the inflamed ducts of his ears, Growing in volume. Then just a few seconds later, the voice of the old man shouting:

'Look at me, boy! Look at me!'

The boy directed his gaze at the place where the old man's voice was coming from and there met his grave eyes, trying desperately to distract him from the sight of the bailiff's shattered head. The goatherd held out his forefinger and pointed at his own eyes. 'Look — at — me,' he said with exaggerated gestures. 'Look — at — me,' he repeated, meanwhile beckoning to him.

The boy crawled over to the goatherd and there, grasping the edge of the table, he managed to stand up with his back to the bailiff. The old man put his hands to the boy's face and the blood from the boy's ears stained his palms. He made the boy turn his head and pressed it against his own broken body. The boy's jaw dropped and trembled as if he were shivering. His eyes empty. The dog poked its nose round the door, but did not come in.

'Let's go.'

Still stunned by what had just happened, the boy took hold of the goatherd's arm and was about to place it round his own shoulders intending to help him walk, but, just then, he saw the bowl of walnuts on the table. He released the goatherd's arm and stood before the bowl. The old man observed him in silence. The boy remained for a while staring at the bowl, his clenched fists resting on the tabletop. Then his head drooped as if his neck had suddenly lost all substance, and he began to sob, a nervous, pent-up sobbing that left him almost unable to breathe. The goatherd let him cry for a while, then placed one hand behind the boy's head and guided him to the door.

In the doorway, the boy dried his eyes on his dirty sleeve, again positioned himself beneath the old man's arm and, together, they went out into the warm, still night. They crossed the small square and headed for the well, the old man dragging his feet, and the boy like a rather feeble crutch supporting the weight of a man who could barely stand. When they reached the well, the boy helped the goatherd sit down with his back against the wall. The crescent moon had still not risen, and it was hard to see further than fifteen or twenty yards ahead. The only source of light was the bailiff's improvised lamp, whose yellowish glow was still percolating out through the open door of the inn. The boy sat down next to the goatherd, and there they stayed, without saying a word, until they fell asleep, leaning one against the other.

★ ★ ★

The boy woke with a start. He had been resting on the old man's bony shoulder, muttering incoherently, when his body gave a sudden jolt and he slumped into the goatherd's lap. He sat up, feeling utterly confused, as if under the influence of ether. He looked at the old man next to him, leaning against the stone wall of the well.

'I was having a bad dream.'

The old man said nothing.

'The bailiff's deputy was trying to burn me.'

'He won't harm you again.'

'What did you do to him?'

'Much the same as I did to his boss.'

The boy put his hands to his ears because he could still hear a kind of whistling coming through his ears via his brain. He glanced around him and could see only stars twinkling above and a half-moon surrounded by a milky aura. There were no signs of life at the inn or anywhere else. A warm breeze blew in from the west, bringing with it the smell of juniper or pine needles.

'Where's Colorao?'

'Don't worry about him now. We have to leave here as soon as possible.'

'Are we going north?'

'Yes.'

'And what will we do when we get there?'

'We've got a long way to go before we have to think about that.'

'I'll go and get the donkey, and then we can leave.'

'Aren't you forgetting something?'

The boy thought for a moment.

'The goats, boy, they're all we have.'

The boy and the dog walked down the middle of the street, heading south. A cat emerged from one of the abandoned houses and walked noiselessly across their path. Just before it reached its destination, the cat stopped and regarded him coolly. Then it continued on its way more slowly this time, and slipped under a door hanging from its hinges.

Just as the goatherd had told him, the donkey was waiting at the entrance to the village, tethered to some railings, and the bailiff's motorbike was parked a little further on. He stroked the donkey's head, feeling its hard angular skull. Then he untethered it, and they left the village and set off to the oak wood.

As they climbed the hill, he could not work out how long he and the goatherd had slept nor how long it would be until dawn, but he knew that he must hurry. He slapped the donkey on the rump a few times, and their pace quickened. Shortly before they reached the wood, the dog ran on ahead and, by the time the boy had got to the corral, he found the three goats running round and round inside with the dog scampering about outside. He removed the undergrowth that had served as a gate and, in a moment, the goats were out, kicking the air. He loaded up the donkey with the old man's belongings and the nearly empty flasks.

They went back down to the village almost at a trot and when they arrived, the boy stopped to study the bailiff's motorbike. He approached it warily. He viewed it with different eyes now. The wide handlebars, the sturdy wheel fork and the curved number plate above the front mudguard like a figurehead. The sidecar with its rounded chassis, the seat in which he had so often been hidden away. He ran his hand over the nose and the windscreen as if he were stroking a horse. Then, leaning in, he saw, on the seat, the blanket with its oilcloth edging and jumped back as if the blanket had suddenly burst into flames. He grabbed the donkey's halter and left as quickly as he could.

When he reached the well, the old man was still sitting where he'd left him. He went over to announce his return and to receive new orders.

'Give the goats some water to drink.'

The boy took one of the flasks from the panniers, poured some water into the bowl and held it to the goatherd's mouth. The man drank the slimy liquid and shot the boy a meaningful glance.

'OK, I'll do the goats next.'

The boy lowered the earthenware pitcher into the well and hauled up some water for the animals and, when they had drunk their fill, he crouched down beside the shepherd.

'Now gather together all the food you can, fill the flasks with water and put them on the donkey.'

'I don't want to go back inside the inn.'

'Would you rather go hungry?'

'I just can't do it. That man . . . '

'He won't do anything to you now, he can't.'

'I'm afraid.'

'Just don't look at his head.'

At the front of the inn, the boy found the bailiff's whip lying on the bench. He picked it up and waved it around as if it were a fly swat. He noticed that the leather on the handle and the stitching were so worn that you could almost see the cane beneath. It ended in a kind of triangular tongue, whose shape the boy had seen before on the old man's body.

He stood at the dark door, brandishing the whip before him. From inside came the familiar meaty aromas as well as a slightly pestilential smell he hadn't noticed before. He leaned blindly into the black room and felt the weight of what had happened in that place. The dense atmosphere of an old sacristy, where the ceremonial robes had been woven at the very beginning of time and where the walls had for centuries absorbed the cries of altar boys, orphans and foundlings. Pain and charity. Death relegated to a corner. Putrefaction now worming its way through unspeakable sins.

He retched and almost vomited. Then he turned and met the eyes of the old man sitting by the well. He took a deep breath, shook his head to clear his mind and, finally, went in, feeling his way along the walls with the whip as his only defence. Dragging his feet so that he didn't step on anything, he reached the place where the meat was hanging. He took half a dozen of the remaining sausages and strung them over his arm.

Having established a route, he brought the donkey to the porch, tethered it to the iron ring on the wall and went back and forth until he had filled all the available space in the panniers with sausages, flour, salt, beans and coffee. When there was no more room, he returned to the well with the donkey and tethered it there. He spent a long time hauling up water and pouring it carefully into the narrow mouths of the flasks. He spilled quite a lot, drenching the panniers and the sides of the donkey which, now and then, reached round to try and lick away this new irritant. Meanwhile, the dog and the goats competed for every trickle.

During all this coming and going, the goatherd had remained leaning against the wall, his head drooping on his chest. When the boy had secured the load with the straps, he covered the whole thing with the blanket, so that the old man could still ride on the donkey's back. He then squatted down beside the goatherd and said:

'I've finished loading the donkey. We can go now.'

The goatherd said nothing, didn't even move, and the boy feared that he was dead. He put his ear to his mouth, but heard nothing. Frightened, he felt the old man's motionless arm. 'Sir,' he said, and the goatherd moved, wearily shaking his grimy head. His eyes opened, and they resembled the dull, worn edges of ancient coins. He murmured something. The boy moved closer, almost pressed his head against the old man's chest and heard those same murmured words.

'Sorry, I didn't understand.'

'You must bury the bodies.'

'What?'

'Bury the bodies.'

The boy stood up and looked around him. The village street was lined with shadows and crumbling walls. The sky kept its usual distance. The boy threw his head back and gave a long outbreath. He felt close to exhaustion and all he wanted at that moment was to return to his hole in the ground, to that warm, damp pit where he had drowsed and slept on the first night of his escape. The primordial hole dug out of our one true mother, the earth. The place where the temperature never changes and where the sun never penetrates and where the roots drill into the clay and hold the soil together against wind and rain. He looked at his trembling hands and sighed. The donkey laden and ready to go, and, beside him, like a troubling reflection, the old man telling him to do something that went entirely against his instincts: burying those bastards, providing them with a safe haven from wild beasts, where they could wait for the final judgement.

The boy again crouched down next to the old man.

'I can't do it alone.'

'You'll have to.'

'There's no spade, no pickaxe.'

'If you don't bury them, the birds will eat them.'

'What does that matter now?'

'It matters.'

'Those men don't deserve it.'

'That's why you must do it.'

★ ★ ★

They agreed that they wouldn't bury the bodies, but would put them somewhere out of reach of dogs and crows. The goatherd explained to the boy where to find the deputy's body and how he should drag him over to join the other two bodies.

'Go to the inn and bring the sack of

chestnuts here. And don't look at the bailiff.'

The boy did as the old man asked and emerged from the inn dragging a sack half filled with chestnuts. Following the goatherd's instructions, he took it over to the donkey, untied the string and, lifting up the blanket, poured part of the contents of the sack into the panniers, with most of the chestnuts slipping into any available gaps among the food, flasks and tools.

With the sack in one hand and the halter in the other, the boy led the donkey over to where the deputy's body was lying on a bench at the back of a derelict house. On the ground, on its side, lay the flask of wine he had taken from the inn. His horse was tethered to a post supporting a withered vine trellis. It pawed the ground nervously when it heard them approach. The boy tried to reassure it by patting its cheek. Thinking that the horse must be thirsty, the boy untethered it in order to take it over to the well, but the horse took fright and galloped off towards the south. The boy regretfully watched it disappear up the hill to the wood. They could have done with a horse like that.

The light from the moon did not reach the place where the body was lying, and the boy could only make out its general shape. The goatherd had told him not to look at the man's head. 'Now that he's dead, you have nothing to fear from him,' he had said, but standing there before the body, the boy felt incapable of doing what he had to do. He imagined the goatherd looming out of the darkness with a stone in his hand.

What the old man did not tell him was that the deputy had been awake when he'd found him. That he was wandering drunkenly around a dusty corral, stumbling over feeding troughs and baskets. That he was singing and praying, his tongue inflamed with drink, and that his face was already the face of a condemned man. Nor did he tell him that, in his drunken delirium, the deputy had confessed everything: the motorbike, the trophy room, the boy's father, the blanket, the silo, the taxes, the Dobermann, the boy. The boys.

Nor did he explain how, after listening to what the deputy had to say he had led him over to the bench and helped him lie down on the hard stone surface. Not a word about his own subsequent rage, not a word about the expiation of sins on a sacrificial altar.

The old man had merely said to the boy that, before he dragged the man's body over to the inn, he must put the sack over his head, like a hood tied around the neck. 'Don't look at the man's face. It will only upset you.'

At first, he resisted approaching the corpse and struggled to manoeuvre the sack. Face averted, he patted the man's lifeless chest, trying to locate the head. He touched something wet on the man's shirt and drew back for a few seconds. Still with eyes averted, he rolled up the mouth of the sack, placed it over the deputy's head and pulled the sack down until it touched the surface on which the body was lying. He then slipped the sack over the man's head until he thought the whole head was inside, then unrolled the sack and tied it around the man's neck with a piece of string. When he was sure the hood would not come off, he pulled hard at the man's legs until the body fell to the ground. On the bench were large gobbets of blackened blood, fragments of brain matter and bleeding remnants of scalp.

He tied the deputy's ankles together and attached the rope to the donkey's halter, as the old man had told him to do. It took a long time to reach the inn, because he had to force the already heavily laden donkey to walk back-wards. When they reached the inn, the boy tried to get the donkey to reverse through the door, but the animal refused, unable to see what lay in the thick darkness behind him.

Outside the door, the boy detached the man's ankles from the donkey's halter and let his feet fall to the ground. He then grabbed his trouser legs and pulled as hard as he could, but he couldn't get the body to move so much as an inch. He tried again several times, but each time he fell back, exhausted, unable to shift it.

There was still no sign of daybreak, but he reckoned that it would not be long before the sun came up. He felt incapable of moving the man's body on his own. For a moment, it seemed to him that it really didn't matter if the man stayed where he was. His quarrel was with the bailiff, not the deputy He looked across at the well. The goatherd was sitting very still, with the dog at his side and the goats scattered nearby. An idea came to him.

He went to the well and hauled up several pitchers of water which he gave to the animals, letting them drink their fill. Then he climbed onto the wall of the well and detached the pulley from the well arch. The sheer weight of it almost made him topple over into the water.

He went back to the inn and put the pulley down on the table. He groped his way along the walls for any store cupboards in which he might find a length of rope. With only the pantry as yet unexplored, he stopped. In the silence, he could hear his own breathing. As he passed the bailiff's body, his boot skidded in the pool of blood coagulating on the floor tiles. To clean the blood off his soles, he scuffed them along the floor as he made his way over to the pantry. With the cripple's stinking body at his feet, he reached out and felt along the shelves, where he found the handles of tools, strings of garlic and a length of rope hanging from a nail.

The chain and manacle of his captivity were still there on the pillar. He managed to hook the pulley onto the manacle, then passed the rope through the rusty wheel. He pulled the two ends of the rope over to the deputy's body and tied one end to the rope around the man's ankles. He then tugged on the other end until the dead man's boots were parallel, as if he were standing to attention. He tried to pull still harder, but the sheer weight of the dead body threw him off balance. Then he rested his feet on either side of the door frame and, using his own weight, pulled again as hard as he could. The corpse moved, only slightly, but it moved. Twenty minutes later, he had managed to winch the deputy far enough into the room to be able to pull the door to.

What he did next was not done on the orders of the goatherd. He went over to the bailiff's body and, keeping his eyes tight shut, patted the man's jacket, feeling for the silver lighter, which, once found, he slipped into his own shirt pocket. He then drenched the bodies with oil from a can he had found in the pantry. The liquid soaked the men's clothes and, when these were saturated, spilled onto the floor, permanently staining the painted tiles. On top of the bodies he scattered wattle fallen from the roof, the rope from the pulley, and the broken wooden crates in which the cripple had kept soda siphons. He picked up the shattered remains of the wicker chair and added them to the pyre, keeping back one slat from which he made a torch by wrapping bits of sacking and cloth around it, secured with twine. Outside, it was beginning to grow light.

The boy returned to the well carrying a wooden crate, and when he got there, squatted down next to the goatherd.

'Everything's ready. We can go now.'

'Are the bodies safe?'

The boy glanced across at the inn, whose whitewashed walls now glowed red in light from the rising sun.

'Yes, I think so.'

'Hell will already have opened its doors to them.'

'It will.'

He placed the straw hat on the old man's head and helped him up. The goatherd scarcely had the strength to stand. His trousers flapped loose about his legs. His ragged jacket barely covered his bruised and beaten body. The boy had not realised until then how very thin the old man was. He helped him sit down on the edge of the wall, placed the wooden crate under his feet and, by pulling on his arms, managed to get him onto the box. Then he brought the donkey over and positioned it sideways on to the goatherd so that the packsaddle and the panniers were at stomach height. The boy helped him lie face down on the load and, by tugging on the old man's arms and legs, finally got him sitting upright on the donkey's back, his legs slotted in between the bulging panniers.

The boy returned to the inn one last time. It was light in the street now, but it would be several hours before the sun penetrated the room. He picked up his improvised torch and peered in, although he could see very little. He breathed in the rancid air and, for the first time, caught the familiar smell of mice. A smell composed of sawdust, nibbled corn grains and chocolate-brown droppings. He could smell the cripple's body, whose insides were doubtless already beginning to putrefy, as well as all the other meaty aromas that still lingered in the atmosphere despite his plunderings. He grabbed the door knocker and pulled hard, but the door wouldn't close. He tried several times without success, then noticed that the deputy's hand was blocking it. He kicked the hand out of the way and this time managed to slam the door shut, listening for the latch to click home. He then looked across at the well and saw the goatherd still mounted on the donkey, head bowed and hands folded submissively like a captive.

He took the lighter from his shirt pocket and flicked it on. The bluish flame illuminated his grimy face. If he could have seen himself in a mirror, he would have burst into tears. He applied the flame to the torch and blew on it until the flame took hold. He held the torch head downwards and turned it slowly until the whole thing was alight. He opened one of the shutters, threw the torch onto the pyre and watched. Nothing happened at first and, for a moment, he feared that the pyre might not catch fire at all and that the torch might burn out. Then, after a couple of minutes, the wicker chair began to burn and the rest followed. Leaving the shutter ajar so that the air would feed the flames, he rejoined the goatherd and the animals. It was daylight by the time he once again took up the donkey's halter and they set off northwards out of the village, heading for the mountains.

11

It wasn't until later in the morning, when they were far from the village and the smoke, that he realised the goatherd was dead. He had decided to stop and rest in a small grove of trees away from the road, because, now that night had passed, it seemed prudent to seek shelter from the sun and from other people, and to try and sleep a little. He thought the goatherd would approve, because that had been the way he himself had organised their journeys, travelling by night and lying low during the day.

This was the first time since they had met that he, rather than the old man, had been the one to decide when they should stop and, in taking that decision, the boy felt that he was now the person in charge and that the old man would perhaps be grateful for his collaboration.

During the journey, he had glanced round several times to make sure that the goats and the old man were all right. At one point, he had noticed that the old man had slumped forward and was actually lying on the necks of the flasks protruding from the panniers.

The boy assumed he had fallen asleep and, knowing how deeply weary the old man must be, he was not surprised that a man his age could maintain such an uncomfortable position.

They left the road and crossed a dry stony stretch of ground. He noticed the tracks they were leaving and felt an impulse to erase them, but although he could brush away the donkey's tracks with branches, he wasn't prepared to go back and pick up all the goats' droppings. He thought about the previous night, about the deputy's crushed skull and the bailiff's head blown to pieces thanks to gunpowder, lead and the goatherd. He thought, too, about the days they had spent travelling, and about the sleepless nights, the hunger and the rare occasions when they had been able to stuff themselves with food. Close now to their destination, he felt his eyelids tremble and, at that precise moment, he really didn't care any more. He could have stopped right there, in the middle of the plain, knelt down and fallen asleep, but they were so very near the wood that he determined to make one last effort.

It was a small pine wood, but dense enough for them to be able to camp inside it and not be seen from the road. Of course, for anyone intent on finding them, it would be easy enough, but, just then, even that did not matter to him. He gathered together a few branches and, using a rough circle of bushes as posts, quickly built a corral of sorts. With the help of the dog, he herded the goats into the corral and went back to help the goatherd dismount and then unload the donkey.

'We can rest here for a while if you like.'

The old man said nothing. The boy went over to the donkey and lifted the brim of the old man's straw hat. His eyes were closed, and the boy rather envied him. He released the goatherd's legs from where they were lodged between the panniers and the donkey's ribcage. Then, propping one shoulder against the old man's waist, he tried to pull him off the back of the donkey. The weight proved too much for him, however, and both of them fell backwards onto the carpet of crisp pine needles.

The old man's body, lying on top of him, stank as much as his. For a moment, the boy couldn't understand what he was doing there underneath, and had it not been for the unbearable stench, he might have stayed there. He pushed at the goatherd, whose body fell back onto the ground like a door opening. He remained there next to the old man's corpse, as if he had thrown off a blanket on a particularly warm morning. Exhaustion bound him to the earth. He lay there, breathing and gazing up at the tops of the pine trees. The millions of needles combed the yellow light and sifted the glow from a sky too bright to be looked at directly. In the breeze the needles kept up a soothing murmur. There was no point shaking the goatherd's head or trying to open his eyelids. The boy knew the goatherd was dead and that was that. He had neither the energy nor the desire to think about what had happened nor about what was to come, because his child's body was utterly exhausted. He shuffled his bottom and his shoulders deeper into the pine needles he was lying on. Then, without thinking, he linked arms with the old man and surrendered to sleep much as someone standing at the seashore allows the wind to cool his face.

★　★　★

He was woken by the dog prodding him in the small of his back. He opened his eyes and touched the dog's head, and the dog immediately relaxed and lay down on the ground. The tops of the pine trees were still there, but they were no longer filtering the intense midday light, and were filled instead with the dusty orange of evening. Suddenly aware of the old man's arm in his, the boy sat bolt upright. His stomach hurt. Something sharp was sticking in his back. He turned, knelt down and scrabbled among the pine needles until he found a small, sharp pine cone. Still rubbing his back, he studied the cone, then lobbed it over the top of the corral. He didn't know how long he had been asleep. The donkey was still there, laden with all the food and implements. The boy went over and pressed his face to the animal's muzzle, stroking its cheeks. Then he emptied the panniers, removed the halter and poured some water into a saucepan he had taken from the inn.

Despite his aching stomach, he walked to the edge of the pine wood to look back at the road. The light was brighter there and, from where he was standing, he saw the road stretching away in either direction. Seeing no sign of movement, he went back to where the old man was lying. The pain in his stomach, he thought, might well be due to the putrid water they'd been drinking, and the only reason his stomach hadn't hurt before was because his body hadn't had a moment's rest. He felt thirsty but, instead of drinking more of the untreated water, he decided that, from then on, he would boil it first. He saw the donkey with its muzzle deep in the saucepan, and his eyes moved from the saucepan to the donkey and then to the goats. He looked around him as if hoping to find some solution in the air around him. A slight breeze to fan a fire or a spring appearing out of nowhere to pour cool water into his leather-dry mouth. Then he felt the bailiff's lighter in his pocket and this decided him against lighting a fire.

He wandered aimlessly about the wood, deliberately avoiding looking at the old man. He checked their store of food, tested the solidity of the frying pan and sniffed the oil. He let the goats out of the corral so that they could move around a little and watched as the dog immediately sprang into action to keep them in order. He again stroked the donkey, went back to the edge of the wood and sat down on a fallen tree trunk. After a while, he remembered that he was thirsty and returned to the encampment.

Choosing the goat with the fullest udder, he sat down behind it and worked the teats with one hand until he had extracted the first few drops. He placed a saucepan underneath and milked until the pan sounded fairly full. He then shooed the goat away and raised the pan to his lips to drink the little milk he had managed to get. He sat still for a while, then put the saucepan down on the ground and went over to where the goatherd was lying. For the first time since the old man had died, the boy dared to look at his corpse. The old man was stretched out on the ground, his face relaxed and seemingly less lined. His straw hat lay about a foot from his body, where it had landed when he fell off the donkey. His fists were almost clenched. His filthy jacket was unbuttoned to reveal the scars from the beating he had taken. He could have been asleep, but he was doubtless already rotting inside. Behind him, the boy heard the clink of goats' bells and, falling to his knees beside the motionless body, he wept.

It was still dark when the ants woke him. They were running over the back of his hand, which served as his pillow, and onto his face. He got to his knees and quickly brushed the ants off. He could barely see six feet in front of him. He touched the old man's body beside him and felt how cold it was. With his hands he scraped away the pine needles until he reached soil and then made a slightly larger clearing. In the centre he piled up a few dry leaves and with the lighter lit a tiny bonfire. The feeble flames were just bright enough for him to be able to see that the goatherd's face and chest were also covered in ants. He got rid of them by using a small pine branch as a broom. He then went to the panniers to fetch the frying pan and stood at the goatherd's feet. Starting at the top of the old man's head, he used the handle of the frying pan to draw a horizontal line out to the left, then he went down to his heels and drew another line. He then extended these lines further out to the left, measured the width of the body with his hands, and transferred that measurement out to the two parallel horizontal lines.

Initially, he made rapid progress. He cleared the pine needles from an area of ground next to the body and, with the help of the frying pan, removed the first layers of sandy soil. A few inches down, however, he encountered roots going in all directions, forming a subterranean fabric in which the frying pan kept getting stuck.

By dawn, the hole he had dug was not even deep enough to cover the old man's nose. Halfway through the morning, he stopped to rest and, from inside the hole, saw that the surrounding earth now came up to his knees. He could have buried him there and then, but any marauding dogs would soon have dug him up. He decided to continue and, by the afternoon, the hole he was standing in came up to his waist.

As on all the previous days, his time was spent either awake or working. Tiredness had become like a second skin. Only one thing occurred to distract him. At midday, the dog got up from its resting place to sniff the air coming from the direction of the road. The boy calmed the dog and led it over to the edge of the wood. A few muleteers were heading north. Three men and ten or twelve pack mules. The boy assumed that they must have passed through the village and would, therefore, know that the inn had been burned down. They would also have seen the bailiff's motorbike at the entrance to the village and would doubtless have found the charred bodies in what remained of the inn.

He pushed the old man's body into the hole, but, as it fell, it turned over and lay face down. The boy gave an angry shake of his head. The hole was so narrow that it took him more than half an hour to turn the body over. Then he gave the old man one last glance before covering his face with a scrap of blanket. He filled the hole with earth until it was level with the ground, scattering any excess soil round about and covering the grave with pine needles. Any dampness left after his excavations would evaporate in a few hours and the grave would be invisible. He remained standing for a while, contemplating the spot where the goatherd lay buried, then he went off in search of something. He returned with a couple of twigs no more than a few inches long and placed them on the ground, one on top of the other, to form a cross. He studied that cross, unable to understand what possible significance those two pieces of wood could have in that grim, remote place. He began to say the Lord's Prayer, but halfway through, the words died on his lips and he stopped. He would have liked to know the old man's name.

He spent what remained of the afternoon resting. He ate whatever he fancied from the panniers and drank as much milk as he could extract from the goats. Then he lay dozing, his head on the panniers and, before it was completely dark, loaded up the donkey, dismantled the corral and set off again. With the Pole Star as guide, they travelled in the moonlight along the flat, empty roads leading north. Sometimes they lost their way, but sooner or later, they always found a path that brought them back so that they were once again heading in the right direction.

One morning, while taking shelter in a run-down old house intended for itinerant road menders, he heard rain drumming on a fallen sheet of corrugated iron. Standing in the dilapidated doorway, he watched the extraordinary spectacle taking place before him. The sky full of grey clouds in the middle of the morning and a transparent light that lent an unfamiliar clarity to the surrounding objects. The fat drops burst on impact with the dusty ground but did not penetrate. He went back into the house and emerged carrying the water pitcher under his arm. He left the pitcher on the ground a few feet away from the house. Then he went back and stood in the doorway for as long as the rain lasted, watching as God temporarily slackened the screws on his torment.

Author's acknowledgements

The author would like to thank Raquel Torres, Arantxa Martínez, Elena Ramírez, Juan María Jiménez, Javier Espada, Espartaco Martínez, Verónica Manrique, Francisco Rabasco, Gustavo González, Fátima Carrasco, María Camón, Diego Álvarez, Germán Díaz, David Picazo and Manuel Pavón.

Carmen Jaramillo deserves a special mention. She improved the book with her enthusiastic support and, by her example, improved the author too.

Translator's acknowledgements

I would like to thank the author for his generosity and patience in answering my many queries and, I am grateful too, as always, to Anella McDermott and Ben Sherriff for all their help and advice.

We do hope that you have enjoyed reading this large print book.

Did you know that all of our titles are available for purchase?

We publish a wide range of high quality large print books including:
Romances, Mysteries, Classics
General Fiction
Non Fiction and Westerns

Special interest titles available in large print are:
The Little Oxford Dictionary
Music Book
Song Book
Hymn Book
Service Book

Also available from us courtesy of Oxford University Press:
Young Readers' Dictionary
(large print edition)
Young Readers' Thesaurus
(large print edition)

For further information or a free brochure, please contact us at:
Ulverscroft Large Print Books Ltd.,
The Green, Bradgate Road, Anstey,
Leicester, LE7 7FU, England.
Tel: (00 44) 0116 236 4325
Fax: (00 44) 0116 234 0205